Pretty Please

The sound of splintering wood and exploding glass mingled with horrified screams and gasps as Jo crashed into and through the door, head first, falling to the stone patio in a shower of flying glass and fragments of wood.

Face down amid the debris, Jo lay perfectly still.

Icy January air rushed into the ballroom.

A stunned silence fell over the crowd. They stood frozen, staring in shock at the patio.

Evan was the first to reach Jo's side. Gently, very gently, he reached down and turned her over.

Someone screamed.

D0544559

NIGHTMARE HALL

Pretty Please

Diane Hoh

■SCHOLASTIC

Scholastic Children's Books,
Commonwealth House, 1–19 New Oxford Street,
London WC1A 1NU, UK
a division of Scholastic Ltd
London~New York~Toronto~Sydney~Auckland

First published in the US by Scholastic Inc., 1994
First published in the UK by Scholastic Ltd, 1996

Copyright © Diane Hoh, 1994

ISBN 0 590 13379 9

Printed by Cox and Wyman Ltd, Reading, Berks

10 9 8 7 6 5 4 3 2 1

Prologue

Several years earlier . . .

It's such a nice day. A pretty day. The sun is shining. I wonder what it would feel like on my face. Warm, I think.

I wish I could go outside. There are other kids out there, I can hear them. They're laughing and shouting and they sound like they're having so much fun. Their school is out for the summer and they're so glad to be on vacation. I wish I could be on vacation with them.

I wonder what it's really like outside? In the daytime, I mean. I wish They'd let me go out before dark.

But I know They're right. If They didn't love me, if They didn't care about me, They'd let me go out. And then everyone would laugh at me and call me names and run away from me. That would hurt so bad. That would hurt more

than it hurts me to look into a mirror. And
that hurts a lot.

I shouldn't complain. It could be a lot worse.
Like They say, I could have been born to people
who didn't care about me, who didn't mind if
I got hurt, people who would let me go outside
and be treated cruelly. I'm very lucky to have
Them. They protect me. They always have.
And They always will.

She said They're getting me a video game for
my eleventh birthday. So I'll have something
new and interesting to do.

I'm really grateful to Them. I love Them
very much. Sometimes I think I hate Them,
but I make those bad thoughts go away.

Because why would I hate Them?

Chapter 1

It should have been a great Friday night. Second semester was underway, it was good to be back on campus after the holidays, Johanna Donahue had a party to attend and a hot new outfit to wear.

What better way to start the new semester? She should have been excited.

But she wasn't. Instead, she found herself moving through the motions of slipping into the new green dress and arranging her long, wavy, auburn hair and applying mascara to her gray-green eyes as if she were slogging through molasses. Every movement took effort.

You would think, she told herself as she applied lip gloss, that I was headed for a final exam instead of a party. What is *wrong* with me?

Something just didn't feel right.

"How about if we blow off this party and

head for a movie instead?" she asked Kelly Benedict, her roommate at Salem U. Kelly, already dressed, was brushing her short, black hair in front of the dresser mirror. "Wouldn't you rather sit through a bad movie than put up with Missy Stark for a whole evening? She's been bragging about giving this party for weeks. But I have a funny feeling about it."

"Are you kidding?" Kelly continued brushing her hair, arranging thick, glossy bangs in a curve over one eye. "I've been slaving for two whole hours to get ready. You want me to waste this on a movie?"

Jo sighed. She hadn't expected Kelly to agree. And it probably was silly. She didn't even know *why* the party seemed, suddenly, like a bad idea. "Like you really needed two hours." Kelly had a natural, fair-skinned beauty that required far less effort than she put into it.

A knock on the door of room 428 Lester dorm was followed by the appearance of a sleek, blonde head. "Okay to come in? I'm ready to be told I look incredibly perfect. Don't disappoint me, guys."

The girl who came in was tall, with long, silky hair and doe-shaped turquoise eyes.

"Well, as usual," Jo said, "you look like you just stepped out of a glamour magazine. A story on How To Look Absolutely Stunning With No Effort At All, featuring Nanette Solomon. It'll sell, Nan, I guarantee it."

"Oh, it takes effort, Jo," Nan said, smiling. "As my mother always said, you don't get something for nothing. I work at it."

"Right." But not very hard, Jo thought. The basics were already there.

"Nan," Kelly said in awe, "*where* did you get that dress? Not here in Twin Falls."

Nan laughed, revealing small, perfect white teeth. "Don't be silly, Kelly. New York, of course." The dress was wine velvet, with a short skirt and a camisole top with tiny spaghetti straps. It suited Nan's cool sophistication perfectly. "You like?" She twirled in front of the roommates.

"I like. You look gorgeous. But," Kelly glanced at Jo, "our friend here is having second thoughts about Missy's party. She's not sure she wants to go."

Nan's perfectly arched eyebrows slid upward. "Why not?"

Jo felt foolish. Why not? She didn't *know* why not. She only knew that for the past couple of hours, a niggling little voice in the back of her head had been saying, don't go, don't go, don't go. . . .

When she didn't answer, Nan added, "What

kind of a party would it be if The Beautiful People didn't show up?"

"Oh, I really *hate* that expression!" Jo sputtered. Someone on campus had bestowed the nickname on the group of five, which included Nan and Kelly's boyfriends, Reed Jameson and Carl Vader, after they'd all modeled for a department store advertisement in the local newspaper. The society editor of the Twin Falls *Gazette* had picked them out of a crowd attending a pre-Thanksgiving football game on campus. The woman had approached them, taken their names, and two days later, Nan had received a phone call. Would she and her friends like to model in a holiday newspaper ad for a local department store?

Yes, they would. It might be fun.

The ad had been so successful it had grown into a series of photo spreads, earning the five a little money and a lot of attention on campus. People still occasionally came up to Jo at a party or basketball game and said, "Hey, weren't you in the newspaper? You're one of The Beautiful People, right?"

Jo still hadn't figured out how to respond to the question. She found it silly and offensive. She hated labels of any kind. They never told much about a person. At least not much of value.

But when she spouted her objections to her friends, they all said the same thing: "Well, it's true, isn't it? We *are* gorgeous, so why should we pretend we aren't?"

Well, yes, it *was* true. Jo knew that. Jo often thought "goddess" when Nan walked into a room, and Kelly was constantly being told she should become a model. Kelly always laughed and said, "Boring, boring," but Jo could tell she was flattered. And Reed and Carl were definitely two of the best-looking guys on campus.

And I'm no slouch, either, Jo admitted to herself as she fastened tiny white snowflake earrings on her lobes. She hadn't been cursed with the freckles and pale lashes of most redheads, her hair was naturally curly, and she'd never needed braces on her teeth. Lucky girl. But she had never thought of herself as "beautiful." In high school, her friends had been average-looking, not asking for a whole lot more than an absence of zits. If they thought about beauty at all, they saw it as something in magazines, on television and in movies, and hoped like mad that it might come to them sometime in the future.

Now, here she was, surrounded by the best-looking people on campus.

The truth was, while all the fuss over their looks sometimes disturbed Jo, she had to admit the attention was kind of fun. Better than being ignored during her first year of college. She had seen those girls on campus . . . the solitary ones, the quiet ones, too shy to make friends, too plain to be noticed. They looked so lonely. It seemed better, by far, to be part of a group with the silly title of The Beautiful People than not to be part of any group at all.

"Never mind," she told Nan. "I'm going to the party. I just had this funny feeling . . ."

With every hair perfectly in place, Kelly turned away from the mirror. "Funny ha-ha, or funny weird?"

"Funny weird. Like . . ." Jo shook her head, "like disaster's waiting in that big, white mansion at the top of the hill."

Kelly and Nan flashed each other a look. Jo knew they thought she was being silly. "Okay, okay, I'm *going*." She'd go and she'd have a good time. Why waste a great new dress on a movie?

Yanking a white wool blazer out of the closet, she slipped it on. "Aren't you two wearing coats? It's January. You'll freeze." Deciding that she might as well get into a party mood, she playfully grabbed a rumpled gray University sweatshirt from the pile of clothing lying on her bed and added with a grin, "Anyone want to borrow this?"

Kelly laughed and wrinkled her nose. "That thing hasn't been washed in a month. Anyway, I have a jacket that goes with this dress." And Nan added, "Mine came with a cape, but it's ugly. Huge gold buttons. I'll grab a coat from my room before we leave."

Reed and Carl arrived a few minutes later.

Compliments about how they looked flowed back and forth. Jo felt oddly detached as she listened, as if she were in an audience watching a play. This was the first act, and the perfectly costumed, perfectly beautiful actors were all in place.

So why couldn't she shake the feeling that an unhappy ending was part of the script?

Telling herself she was being ridiculous, Jo grabbed her clutch bag. She'd be fine once she got to the party. The feeling would go away and she'd have a great time, as always.

It should have worked out that way. Jo wasn't wild about Missy Stark, who was fond of bragging about her father, the head of the foreign studies department at Salem, but she was willing to admit that Missy threw a great party. Dr. Stark had married a woman with both money and taste, and the impressive Stark mansion, high on a hill overlooking the village of Twin Falls, was brightly lit, warm, and welcoming.

But when they walked into the huge white house and were immediately surrounded by friends and good music and great food, the sense of relief Jo had been expecting didn't come. She still felt as if she were watching from a distance, watching and . . . waiting. . . .

Chapter 2

Kelly dragged Reed off to explore the mansion, and Nan and Carl drifted off to the ballroom to dance. In an effort to avoid her hostess, who was running around the house armed with a camera and eager to use it, Jo sought refuge in the library.

She had never seen so many books. Floor-to-ceiling shelves, all the way around the huge, Persian-carpeted room. Heavy maroon draperies blanketed the windows, and a roaring fire blazed in the huge, wood-paneled fireplace centered in the far wall.

It was too tempting. Maybe in this welcoming room, she could ease out of the unexplained anxiety she felt, like a snake shedding its skin. Then she could have a good time, like everybody else.

"Couldn't deal with it, hmm?" a deep voice said as she rounded a corner of the high-backed, cream-colored couch to approach the fireplace. "Can't blame you. I had enough five minutes after I walked into this showplace."

The voice came from the couch. Lying there was a tall leggy guy in a pair of jeans and a blue plaid flannel shirt. He had a thin, angular face, a thick crop of coffee-colored hair, and blue eyes under thick brows. The lips were slightly curved in an amused half-smile.

He wasn't as model-gorgeous as Carl or Reed. But Jo liked that smile.

"I didn't know anyone was in here," she said defensively, backing away from the couch.

He sat up. "I wasn't accusing you of anything. I was complimenting you on having the good sense to escape that zoo out there. I'd bet my scholarship you were wishing you were somewhere else, right? Of course I'm right."

Maybe. But he couldn't know the reason. She probably looked perfectly normal from the outside, not at all like someone whose nerves were all tied up in knots and didn't know why.

He stood up. "Evan Colt. And you are . . . ?"

"Johanna Donahue," she managed, her voice stiff. "And I'm leaving now."

But when she turned to go, he reached out and stopped her, his hand on her left elbow. "No," he said, "I don't think so." He smiled fully then, and it seemed to Jo that someone had suddenly ripped all of the heavy draperies from the windows and let in a warm, bright sun. "I told myself while I was relaxing on that couch that if a girl with the good sense to leave that dull crowd walked in here, I'd want to know her. I just didn't expect her to look like you. Talk to me. Do people call you Johanna or do they corrupt it into something shorter?"

"Jo," she said shortly. Maybe she should give him a chance. He was, after all, the kind of person who had sought out the peace and quiet of the library, just as she had. That had to mean something.

When he took her hand and led her to a seat on the couch, she didn't protest. Talking to someone new and interesting might shake her feeling that she really wasn't present at this party, that she was watching from a distance, and waiting. . . .

It was worth a try.

And, for a little while, it worked. Evan *was* interesting. She liked to watch the expressions on his face change from a lighthearted smile to an annoyed frown, which happened often as he spoke. It was a great face, strong-boned and well-designed, like something chiseled on a mountainside.

She liked the way he moved, light and easy

on his feet, when he got up to stir the fireplace embers with a poker.

But when he asked her if she was interested in dancing and they left the library to join other couples dancing in the ballroom, the feeling of anxiety swept over her again like a cold fog.

She didn't understand it. The music was great, she was surrounded by friends, and she was with a new and interesting person. And as they walked past the glass patio doors, she saw her reflection. The image was that of a very pretty girl with long auburn hair, wearing a green dress, dancing with a tall, good-looking guy.

Perfection.

She should have been having the time of her life, and instead there were tiny little insects of worry crawling up and down her spine. What on earth was *wrong* with her?

I don't *get* like this, she puzzled as she and Evan danced. I'm not the nervous type and I don't get anxious in thunderstorms and I'm not the least bit afraid of the dark. So what is my problem tonight?

She *did* think it was funny when Kelly and Reed walked into the ballroom and saw her dancing with Evan. Kelly's perfect jaw actually dropped, and her elbow made a beeline for Reed's ribs, alerting him. He, too, looked surprised when he saw Jo with Evan.

Well, for pete's sake, she thought, you'd think they'd never seen me with a guy! I've had plenty of dates since I got to Salem.

And then it occurred to her that what was probably surprising her friends was not that she was with a guy, but how *happy* she looked about being with this particular one. It was a look they hadn't seen before.

Well, she thought, at least I *look* like I'm relaxed. My sudden attack of unexplained paranoia isn't showing. That's a relief.

She noticed then, sitting alone in a chair along one wall, a tall, thin, plain girl with straight blonde hair. It was the look in the girl's eyes as she watched the dancers that tugged at Jo's heart. She didn't know the girl, but she could see how desperately she wanted to be a part of the scene instead of being a spectator.

That's the way I felt earlier, Jo thought as the song ended, as if I were part of the audience instead of being *in* the play. It wasn't a good feeling. That girl has probably felt like part of the audience ever since she got to Salem.

What was it like to always be on the outside looking in? Even in high school she hadn't felt that way.

I don't ever want to know, Jo thought emphatically.

They were about to go forage for food at one of the long, narrow, white-clothed tables lining the walls when Missy, camera in hand, stopped them.

"You are not taking one more step until I get your picture," she said archly. "I bought a special album, just for pictures of this party. And you've been avoiding me all night long, Johanna." Then she added snidely, "I suppose posing isn't as much fun when you're not getting paid."

Evan looked surprised. "You're a model?" he asked.

Jo shook her head, annoyed with Missy, but relieved that Evan hadn't known about the newspaper ads. For a while after the ads started, they'd all been besieged by phone calls and notes from admirers. She was glad Evan hadn't been one of them.

"Look," Missy said, "I insist on getting a picture of The Beautiful People — at *my* party."

Jo sighed. "Oh, all right. Wait'll I grab the others and we'll pose for *one* picture, Missy, that's all. Just one, so you'd better do it right."

She dragged Evan with her as she moved around the ballroom collecting Kelly and Nan, Reed, and Carl.

"What's our fee?" Carl asked jokingly, and

Reed, who had just filled a plate with food, groaned at being interrupted.

"Put the plate down, Reed," Jo warned, "or Missy will run over and snatch it right out of your hands. She means business." She grinned as Reed reluctantly put the plate back on the table. "It's hard being gorgeous, isn't it, Reed? So many obligations. . . ."

Evan laughed.

In spite of her eagerness, it took Missy an intolerable length of time to decide where they should pose. She finally decided on a long, narrow bench to the left of the glass patio doors. "Females in front, on the bench," she ordered, "guys in back, standing. That way I can get you all in at the same time."

Evan, who had refused to pose with them and received no argument from Missy, stood off to one side. "Those candles over their heads are going to cast shadows on their faces," he pointed out.

Missy barely glanced at the pair of burning candelabra, sitting on shelves above the bench. "It'll be romantic," she said, peering into her camera. "A nice, romantic glow. Just the effect I want."

It hasn't been a bad night at all, Jo thought, straightening her skirt and obediently sitting up straight on the bench. Not bad at all. I think

I have finally relaxed. Whatever that nagging feeling was, it must have come from something I ate.

She wet her lips as she'd been taught to do and prepared to smile when Missy said "Cheese!" Although in Missy's case, she might well say "petit fours" or "caviar."

A crowd had gathered to watch them pose. Missy was calling out orders like a drill sergeant — sit this way; move that way; turn in this direction; take a step backward, Reed; cross your legs, Nan — when a couple came in through the patio doors, bringing a sudden gust of wind with them.

The wind circled the bench. The group shivered with the sudden cold.

Missy, annoyed, lowered the camera.

Then the wind danced on, wrapping itself around the candelabra on the wall behind the bench. The wind pulled and tugged at the flames, teasing them, fueling them into two separate, roaring blazes shooting out of the wall.

Someone slammed the glass doors shut.

With a disappointed moan, the wind died.

But before Missy could lift the camera again, a girl in the crowd of onlookers gasped and screamed, "Reed's jacket's on fire!"

The three girls on the bench jumped up and whirled around.

There were no flames, only smoke behind Reed's head, but it was clear that his jacket had been touched by the brief, sudden blaze. It was also clear that the cloth could burst into flames at any moment.

Reed's eyes were startled, his face as stark-white as the wall behind him. "What should I do?" he whispered.

Everyone began screaming at once. "Throw him on the floor! Back him up against the wall! Someone get a blanket!"

The crowd surged forward, pushing Jo aside.

It was Evan who shouted, "Take the stupid jacket off!"

Too late. The jacket burst into flames. Yellow and orange spires shot up into the air and singed Reed's hair, causing him to cry out. His eyes were wild with fear.

Jo's only thought as she watched, horrified, was to get to her friend's aid and rip the jacket off him before he was seriously injured.

She tried to move forward; to join Carl, struggling to remove the flaming jacket from a fear-paralyzed Reed.

But the crowd, a solid wall of people bordering on hysteria caused by the sight of the flames, surrounded her, imprisoning her.

Jo pushed against them, pushed hard.

Just as she thought she was going to break free, that one more step would do it, something hit the small of her back, hard, knocking her off-balance.

At the same moment, the crowd surged forward. With nothing solid to grasp and no one in front of her to break her fall, Jo was slammed forward as if she'd been hit by a truck.

She was thrown directly into one of the glass doors.

The sound of splintering wood and exploding glass mingled with horrified screams and gasps as Jo crashed into and through the door, head first, falling to the stone patio in a shower of flying glass and fragments of wood.

Face down amid the debris, Jo lay perfectly still.

Icy January air rushed into the ballroom.

Behind her, Reed's jacket, safely off him, lay smoldering on the floor.

A stunned silence fell over the crowd. They stood frozen, staring in renewed shock at the patio.

Evan was the first to reach Jo's side. Gently, very gently, he reached down and turned her over.

Someone screamed.

Johanna Donahue's beautiful face was smeared from forehead to chin with bright red blood.

Chapter 3

When Jo woke up, she was surrounded by white. It took her several dazed moments to realize she was lying in one of the small white cubicles in the infirmary. She had been there once before, when she'd been struck in the head by a softball early in the first semester.

A tall, blonde woman in a white jacket, clipboard in hand, was standing at the foot of her bed. Her name, Jo remembered, was Dr. Trent.

"Well, you're awake! Good." The doctor moved around to stand beside Jo. "I have good news for you. No serious harm done."

Jo worked at sorting things out. The party . . . Reed's jacket on fire . . . the glass doors . . . she had fallen . . . Jo gasped. She'd gone through those doors headfirst. The glass had exploded . . . her hands flew to her face. Had it been sliced to ribbons by that flying glass?

She felt bandages — lots of tape and a thick pad of gauze under one eye. "Oh, no!" she cried. "What's happened to my face?"

"You're fine," Dr. Trent said. "Don't let the bandages scare you. You've only got one serious cut on the side of your neck, where a scar won't show, and another less serious one on your right cheek, just under your eye. You were very lucky."

Lucky? Fighting tears, Jo gingerly explored the patchwork of tiny pieces of tape and the larger squares of gauze, one on her neck, one on her cheek. She felt like a mummy. Her heart sank and she struggled against panic. No one would be asking her to model for newspaper ads any time soon.

"I notified your mother," the doctor said. "I explained that you're not in any danger, and I think she's okay with it. But I'm sure she'd like to hear from you. Give her a call as soon as you're fully awake, okay? There's a phone on the wall over there."

When Jo had pulled herself together, she made the call, assuring her mother that there was no need for a visit to campus. She sounded much more certain than she felt. Her face felt stiff and sore. How could she be sure the doctor was telling the truth about no serious damage?

Couldn't she just be saying that so Jo wouldn't get hysterical?

She wanted to find a mirror and check for herself.

Then, just as quickly, she decided she *didn't* want to find a mirror. Not yet.

She decided that she would believe the doctor. "No serious harm done." She would believe it because she couldn't stand not to.

Her friends were allowed to see her, and they all breathed a heavy sigh of relief when the doctor informed them that "It's not as bad as it looks, I promise." She smiled at the white-faced group anxiously gathered around Jo's bed. "I know all that blood must have been scary," she said, "but most of the cuts were surface lacerations. I only had to stitch two, and one of those was on the side of her neck. It will hardly show at all."

"She's going to look," the doctor continued, "like she tangled with a tiger, for a couple of weeks. After that, she should be good as new. I'm going to keep her here overnight to watch for any signs of a head injury. But my take on it is that she'll be free to go in the morning. Stop by then."

They wanted to believe the doctor. But Jo could see that they were skeptical. She didn't blame them. Even without a mirror, she could imagine what she looked like.

"Is Reed okay?" she asked anxiously.

Evan nodded. "The hair on the back of his neck was singed, but that's about it. I think he's still shaking, though. We took him home and put him to bed."

They had all had a terrible scare. And Jo could see that they hadn't quite recovered from it yet. Nan and Kelly were white as sheets, and Carl was staring at her as if he expected her to burst into tears at any moment.

What good would that do? She'd just get her bandages wet.

Although she was given something to help her sleep, she spent a long, restless night, tossing and turning and trying to tell herself that her face wasn't her most important asset. There were other things, good things, that had nothing to do with her appearance.

But . . . her face was what people saw *first*. So it mattered, no matter how hard she tried to pretend it didn't.

She fell asleep and dreamed of the newspaper ads they'd posed for. But in her dream, there were only four people in all of the photos. She was missing. And when she complained to the editor, he smiled at her and said, "Well, of course you're not in them. You're no longer one of The Beautiful People, not with *that* face."

She woke up chilled and shaking, and had a hard time going back to sleep.

The following morning, when her friends, including Reed, showed up to take Jo back to Lester dorm, their skepticism was obvious. Reed, who hadn't seen her the night before, looked especially shocked. Because the patient really did look, as the doctor had warned them, as if she had "tangled with a tiger." And she *didn't* look as if she'd be "good as new" any time soon.

Her face was a patchwork quilt of bruises and cuts, which peeked out from beneath the bandages that crisscrossed her face and neck.

Jo had decided, upon awakening after her bad night, that she was going to take things one day at a time. No point in getting all bent out of shape over this until she knew for sure that she wouldn't have to wear a bag over her head for the rest of her life.

"I know, I know," she said, gingerly attempting a grin. "I'm not looking my best." Already dressed in the clothes Kelly had brought her the night before, she stood up. "But it could have been a lot worse, right?"

When no one said anything, Jo laughed nervously. "It *could* have, right?"

Then they all murmured, "Sure, of course,

it's not that bad." But their eyes still registered shock. After what the doctor had told them the night before, they had been expecting Jo to look almost normal.

She did not, she knew, look almost normal. Probably not even close.

Sensing their discomfort, Jo babbled nervously all the way to the dorm. "I'm glad I only had to stay one night," she said, trying valiantly to ignore the blatant stares of people who passed them on the Commons, a grassy area surrounded by tall stone and brick ivy-covered buildings. Some people actually stopped in their tracks, eyes wide, as Jo passed by. "That place is too noisy. They were working on that new wall behind the infirmary at six o'clock this morning. Six o'clock!"

Groups of people whispered and sneaked quick glances at Jo, avoiding eye contact. Their horror showed plainly on their faces.

Jo felt her aching face flush with heat. How could people be so *rude*?

And was this kind of awful attention what was in store for her? She was used to positive attention. Admiring glances. Not this . . . this shocked curiosity, as if she were an exhibit in a freak show.

She'd never be able to stand it.

They passed a pair of Twin Falls policemen,

walking toward Butler Hall, the administration building.

"What are they doing here?" Jo asked Evan.

He shrugged. "Who knows? Complaining about too many speeding tickets being doled out to our fellow students, maybe?"

"I think," Nan said, "they're here about some girl who disappeared."

"Disappeared?"

"Well, she's gone. A freshman. Hasn't been to class or slept in her bed, I heard. She probably just went back home. Let's face it, everyone doesn't love Salem the way we do, right?"

"Who is she?" Jo asked. "Anyone we know?"

"Not really," Nan replied. "At least, I didn't. Sharon Westover." Her tone of voice implied that anyone she didn't know couldn't be all that important. Nan had very clear ideas about who mattered and who didn't. Someone she didn't know didn't matter. "The girl who was in that bad car wreck last fall. I heard she'd been depressed ever since. So she probably just took off, right?"

"Look," Carl told Jo, "you've got enough to worry about. Don't start obsessing about people you don't even know. Nan's probably right, anyway. The girl decided to go home and work at the local fast food joint." He laughed. "I've thought about it a couple of times, especially around finals."

Jo decided Carl was right. What was she doing worrying about someone she didn't even know when every inch of her face stung?

People were still staring.

Lowering her head, she hurried her steps. And changed the subject. "So," she said, her voice unnaturally high, "is Missy worried that I'm going to sue? Or is she just going to send me a bill for the patio door?" Her laugh, too, was high and strained. "I don't usually destroy houses I'm partying in."

They all laughed then, and that helped. By the time they reached room 428 at Lester, they were all laughing and talking, as if nothing horrible had happened.

"We didn't have time to get balloons or flowers," Kelly apologized as she held the door open for Jo. "But I did go downstairs and get you a Coke and a glazed doughnut."

The snack was sitting on the table beside Jo's bed.

"That's exactly what I was hoping for," Jo said, smiling and heading for the bed. "Thanks, Kelly."

Reaching for the Coke, she had her back to the room when she heard a soft "oooh" of dismay behind her. Evan said, "What . . . ?" and Carl let out a soft whistle.

Jo turned around.

Her eyes followed their stunned gaze . . . to the wide, framed mirror hanging over the large wooden dresser Jo and Kelly shared.

The mirror was completely draped in black.

Chapter 4

Jo stared at the mirror, which was covered from side to side and top to bottom with heavy black fabric. Not an inch of glass showed. When she found her voice, she questioned, "Kelly?"

Kelly was staring at it, too. "Jo, I . . ." She tried again. "I . . . it wasn't like this when I left the room to go downstairs. It *wasn't*. I . . . I wouldn't do this."

Jo looked at her roommate. "You didn't do this? You weren't trying to . . . protect me?"

"Protect you? Jo, I do *not* think of you as needing my protection. Not even after last night. I know lots of people who would steer clear of mirrors if they'd been . . . banged up like you have. But you're not one of them. I didn't *do* this."

"It's a joke," Carl suggested, moving forward to tug at the black fabric. "A sick joke,

I'll give you that, but it's got to be a joke. Maybe Missy did it."

"Nah." Reed shook his head. "This isn't her kind of thing. Besides, she probably took to her bed because her party was a disaster. We won't see her on campus for at least three days, I guarantee it."

Carl was still tugging on the fabric. "Well, whoever did it," he said, "did a good job. This stuff wasn't just tossed over the mirror. It was *glued* on. Anybody got a knife?"

Evan had a pocketknife. Opening the blade, he began to cut away the black fabric.

Jo went over and sat down on her bed. She felt sick. "Do I really look that bad?" she asked quietly, her eyes on the floor. "All those people were staring at me . . ."

They all rushed to reassure her. "Of course not, Jo. You look fine. Don't be silly, Jo."

But *someone* thought she looked that bad. *Someone* thought she shouldn't even look into a mirror.

When Evan had stripped away the last of the fabric, he glanced around the room. "You guys have your own bathroom?" he asked.

Kelly nodded, waving a hand toward the bathroom. "Why?" Then her face paled and she whispered, "Oh, no . . ."

Evan, his mouth set grimly, turned in the direction of Kelly's wave.

But Jo jumped up and ran to the bathroom doorway before anyone could stop her. When she looked inside, one hand flew to her mouth. The mirror on the medicine cabinet was draped exactly as the dresser mirror had been. "Oh, I don't believe this," she said softly. "What is going *on?*"

Evan hurried over to gently move her away from the door. "Go sit down," he said. "I'll get rid of it." And he disappeared inside, closing the door behind him.

No one said anything as Jo, tears beginning to slide down her cheeks, returned to sink down upon her bed. Kelly joined her, putting a comforting arm around Jo's shoulders. "Someone on campus has a really sick sense of humor," Reed said awkwardly, leaning against the dresser. "Don't let it throw you, Jo, okay?"

Jo glared at him. Easy for *him* to say. *His* face didn't look like he'd been run over by a lawnmower. There was no visible damage at all from the fire the night before. He was as gorgeous as ever. Still, Reed was only trying to be nice.

Evan came out of the bathroom, his hands filled with a bundle of black. "I'll get rid of this," he offered, and left the room.

"How well do you know that guy?" Carl asked when the door had closed.

Jo looked up at him. "What?"

"Well, I mean, you just met him, right? Last night?"

Jo nodded.

"Did he seem like the kind of guy who would go in for practical jokes? *Creepy* practical jokes, for instance?"

Jo was about to retort, Don't be ridiculous, when she realized that she couldn't. After all, how much *did* she know about Evan? Almost nothing.

"It's just that he *did* ask about the bathroom mirror," Carl continued. "None of the rest of us even thought about a second mirror. It was almost like . . . like he *knew*."

Jo wanted more than anything to say, No, you're wrong, Carl. It couldn't have been Evan. But she was too hurt and confused to say anything.

Evan returned to a roomful of silence. He picked up on it right away. "Sorry, folks, but you've got the wrong guy," he said drily. "I know I'm the new kid on the block in this group. But I'm also the only one here who didn't know Jo's room number."

"Anyone can get a room number," Carl said stubbornly. "Piece of cake."

Evan smiled lazily. "This is true. But that 'anyone' would have to have a reason to make Jo miserable." He looked at Jo. "Making Jo miserable isn't on my agenda. You can take my word for that or not, your choice. But I think a better idea would be figuring out who *does* want to make Jo miserable."

Jo felt her lacerated face grow warm as Evan smiled at her.

"I think Carl was right in the first place," Kelly said, patting Jo's arm consolingly. "It has to be a joke. An awful one, but still . . . maybe one of Missy's friends did it."

Nan nodded agreement. "Look, I've got a newspaper meeting. Carl, you're due there, too. Anyway, we should go and let Jo get some rest. Remember," waving a finger at Jo, "the doctor said you're supposed to stay in bed today and tomorrow. And take your pain medication, okay? Don't try and tough this out when you can take a pill and sleep."

"Yes, mother."

"I should go, too," Kelly said reluctantly. "I'm supposed to meet Cath Devon at the mall to get stuff for her party next week, but I hate leaving you here all alone. Are you going to take your pill and go to sleep? If you're not, I'll stay."

"I don't need a baby-sitter," Jo said. Then,

in a gentler tone, "Go ahead and go. Bring me back a magazine? I promise I'll do as I'm told, like the good girl that I am. Go on. How can I get any sleep if you're hovering all over me? But," she added lightly, "you might want to lock the door when you leave, okay? So . . . so no one will barge in and wake me up."

Saying he would call her later, Evan left with the others.

When they had gone, Jo sat on the bed, her hands folded in her lap. Her face stung like crazy. She would take her pill and crawl under the covers and go to sleep, forgetting all about the cruel mirror joke.

But for the first time since she had arrived on campus in late August, Jo wasn't comfortable in her own room.

The cozy room that had felt like home to her since the day she'd moved in now seemed suddenly different.

Jo looked around at the collages of high school mementoes over each bed, the brightly colored plastic trays of accessories, the collection of patchwork-quilted toss pillows Kelly had bought at the mall.

The knowledge that someone had been in there, someone who clearly wasn't a friend, someone who had no *right* to be in their room, that changed everything.

Violated, Jo thought angrily, I feel violated. Even though whoever it was hadn't touched anything except the mirrors. . . . They hadn't, *had* they? Jo glanced around the room again quickly, looking for opened drawers or suspicious disarray. No, they hadn't touched anything else as far as she could tell.

Nevertheless, they had been *in* there. She hated that.

She made sure the door was locked before taking her pill and climbing into bed. In the bathroom, as she filled a glass of water, she bent low over the sink to avoid meeting her own eyes in the mirror. The mirror . . . how could she ever look at that mirror again without remembering the black shroud draped over it?

Maybe, she thought despairingly as the pill began to take hold, maybe I won't ever *want* to look in a mirror again.

Because in spite of what the doctor and her friends had said to reassure her, there *was* someone on campus who thought she looked so awful, she shouldn't even think about looking into mirrors.

What if that person was right?

When Jo finally drifted off to sleep, she dreamed that she was receiving her degree at a graduation ceremony outside on the Commons on a beautiful, sunny, blue-skied day in June.

But when she went up on stage to receive the rolled scroll tied with a ribbon, and turned to smile at the audience seated on folding chairs, she had no face.

There was only a blank oval where her features should have been.

Chapter 5

She'll never be the same. Never.

She was so pretty. Beautiful, really. Although she didn't even seem to realize it. She had a flawless face. Flawless.

But not anymore.

Now there's no choice. Can't have her running around in public scaring people. Even when the bandages come off, she'll have those horrible black stitches running up and down her face. And the scars. Gives me the creeps just thinking about it.

This is going to be hard, though. I wouldn't mind so much if Johanna were ordinary. But she's not. She's different. Special. The minute I saw her, I knew I had to get to know her. Too bad. Too, too bad.

Can't help it. Not her fault, not my fault, it's just the way it is. I can't ignore my mission. That would be wrong.

I don't have to do it immediately. If only she'll keep her face covered so no one can see it. I can wait.

But if she doesn't, I'll have no choice.

Chapter 6

Jo went to her classes on Monday. People stared and murmured or whispered behind their hands each time she walked into a lecture hall. She had tried to prepare herself for the attention, but soon found that it wasn't that easy. Maybe her friends were too kind to be honest with her about how bad she really looked.

She had looked in the mirror half a dozen times that morning while dressing. Slipped carefully into a cranberry turtleneck sweater, mindful of her bandages . . . and looked in the dresser mirror. Told herself she didn't look that bad. Pulled on a pair of jeans, zipped the zipper, slid a leather belt into the loops . . . and looked in the mirror. *Tried* to tell herself she'd seen worse. Pushed her feet into black suede boots, fastened a gold chain around her neck . . . and looked in the mirror. Hoping, as she had each time before, that her appearance would miraculously have changed . . . improved . . . the cuts and bandages gone, her skin smooth and clear again.

Didn't happen.

So she had taken a deep breath, brushed her thick, wavy hair away from her face, carefully applied mascara, picked up her books, slipped into a jacket, and left the room, giving her bed one last, longing glance as she closed the door. Staying in bed one more day would give her twenty-four more hours to gear up for the stares and whispers. And no one would blame her. She had a right, just now, to pamper herself.

But she couldn't do it. Missing a whole day of classes was no way to begin a new semester.

Of course, having your face destroyed by a glass door wasn't such a great way to start off, either.

Jo had stepped into the dorm's fourth floor elevator with a churning stomach.

After three hours of classes, her stomach was still churning. She hadn't seen Evan or any of her other friends all morning. Maybe they were avoiding her. *If only Missy hadn't made us pose for that ridiculous picture,* Jo thought for the thousandth time as she left the lecture hall. *The only thing I could pose for now is one* of those Safety First ads. The caption underneath my picture could read, OPEN ALL GLASS DOORS BEFORE EXITING.

Jo was pleasantly surprised to find Evan waiting for her outside. "Nice colors," he commented as she smiled a hello.

Jo glanced down at her sweater. "Thanks."

"Not your clothes. Your face. It's turning a veritable rainbow of purples and blues. There's even a little yellow tossed in for good measure."

Jo surprised herself by laughing.

"Great," Evan said, putting an arm around her shoulders. "I knew I was right about you. There are two kinds of people in this world. Those who whine and those who laugh. I knew when you walked into Missy's library that you weren't a whiner. You just confirmed that."

The praise warmed her. And made her feel a little less self-conscious. "It just so happens," she said archly, "that I am in great pain. Tremendous pain. I've never *been* in so much pain. And I expect you to give me the sympathy I deserve."

Evan groaned. "Oh, great! A whiner! How could I have been so wrong? This is a critical blow to my powers of observation." Then, as they began walking down the wide hall, he changed his tone of voice. "You're not really in a lot of pain, are you?"

"No. At least not physically. But I'm not wild about being the center of so much attention."

"You should be used to it. Don't forget, Jo, I saw your face *before* your close encounter with that door. Definitely the kind of face people stare at. I know *I* must have been staring. You probably just never noticed."

"Well, I'm noticing *now*. And I hate it."

It was even worse in the dining hall at Lester. It was already crowded when they walked in. A sudden silence fell over the crowd and Jo knew it wasn't because everyone had, at that precise moment, lost their powers of speech.

"Oboy," she breathed.

Evan gripped her elbow firmly and, whispering encouragement in her ear, led her forward to the cafeteria line.

At least, while on line, she had her back to the room. That was a relief.

Kelly and Reed waved to them from the back of the room.

Jo deliberately held her head up all the way across the hall, fighting a forceful urge to hide behind Evan's height and wide shoulders.

She shut her ears to the whispering and closed her eyes against the stares.

An awkward hush settled over the long, narrow table as Jo and Evan set their trays down.

Her face felt as if it were on fire as she slid into her chair.

Then Carl said loudly and cheerfully, "Hey, Jo, wrestled any tigers today?"

Over the horrified gasps that followed his comment, Jo grinned and said, "You think it's easy to find a tiger to wrestle? Listen, Carl, tigers are in short supply at this university."

Everyone at the table laughed, and the atmosphere eased considerably.

Almost everyone. Jo couldn't help noticing that Reed and Kelly hadn't even cracked a smile. Kelly's usually pink skin was marble-white.

"I don't see how you can joke about this," she whispered across the table to Jo. "It really isn't the least bit funny."

Reed nodded, and bit down hard on a carrot stick.

"Oh, Kelly," Jo said, "it's either laugh or cry. And if I cry, I'll get my bandages wet and they'll flop off, and then everyone will run screaming from the dining hall."

Kelly winced, clearly upset by the mental picture of Jo's face, unbandaged.

Nan, sitting a few chairs away, asked, "So, are you going to need plastic surgery? My mother knows this great doctor in Tucson. For a small fortune, he keeps her looking thirty years old. Want me to get his name?"

Jo shook her head. "First of all, I don't *have* a small fortune. Second, I'm not going to need major reconstruction. One or two little scars aren't going to ruin my life. The modeling was fun, but it's not as if I were planning that for my career. I'm pre-med, remember?"

Kelly and Reed, still unsmiling, got up and left, saying they had classes. Nan and Carl followed soon after, leaving Jo and Evan flanked by empty seats.

"Alone at last!" he said, smiling. "So, did you hear about that costume party at Nightmare Hall Friday night?"

Jo knew about the party. It was being given by Cath Devon, a resident of an off-campus dorm, Nightingale Hall, just down the road from the university. A huge, old brick house set high up on a hill under a canopy of dark oak trees, it had been nicknamed Nightmare Hall after a young girl had mysteriously died there. Although the mystery had eventually been solved, the nickname remained.

"I hate costume parties," Jo complained.

"Look at it this way," Evan said, teasing, "you can wear a mask."

Jo brightened considerably. "Hey, I hadn't thought of that! Let's see, I can wrap myself entirely in white bandages and go as a mummy.

Or I could get one of those white hockey masks like Jason wears in the *Friday the 13th* movies."

"You have many different options," Evan said with great solemnity. "So, how about if we go together?" He smiled hopefully.

"Sounds great."

Lunch with Evan distracted Jo. She was finally able to forget about her face. But as she walked to her first afternoon class, it started all over again, the stares, the whispering.

By the time she was seated in math class, her nerves were singing again. Would this day *never* end?

Maybe people would get used to her bandages after a day or two. Something more interesting would come along to divert their attention. She'd be yesterday's news. And in a couple of weeks, the bandages were coming off, anyway.

Two girls behind her were whispering like mad, and when she turned her head to shoot them an annoyed glance, she found their eyes riveted on her.

Thoroughly discomfited, Jo found herself reaching into her purse for her compact. Maybe one of the pieces of tape had come loose. She should have stopped in the restroom after lunch and checked.

It took her a while to dredge up her compact from the depths of her oversized leather shoulderbag. When her fingers finally closed around the round plastic compact, she slipped it out of the bag as surreptitiously as possible. She didn't want the two girls, still busily whispering back there, to know they'd forced her to check her face in a mirror. She hated to give them that much satisfaction.

Laying the compact on top of her textbook, Jo flipped it open.

Her jaw dropped and a soft, startled, "Uh" slid out from between her lips.

In the round circle that should have been reflecting her face, there was only . . . *black*. Like the mirrors in her room, the glass in Jo's compact was completely covered with a small, perfectly round swatch of thick black fabric.

Not an inch of glass was visible.

Chapter 7

Jo's right hand shook as she reached out slowly and used one finger to pick at the black fabric, as if she were scratching a mosquito bite. The cloth remained firmly in place.

Glued. Just like on the mirrors in her room.

She began shaking so violently, the compact slid off her book and fell to the floor with a sharp rap.

The boy sitting behind her leaned forward to whisper, "You okay? You're rocking my seat like an earthquake." Then, when Jo didn't answer, he complained, "Hey, you're knocking everything off my desk!"

Pencils hit the floor and rolled.

But Jo couldn't stop shaking.

Everything became a blur after that. Someone came to stand beside her desk, bending to look into her face, asking her something, then lifting her. And then another someone whose face she didn't remember helped her out of the room, down the hall, across campus.

The next thing she was aware of was being back in the infirmary, surrounded by white walls and the noise from the construction going on outside. The doctor's kind, concerned face was looking into hers. She was asking Jo something. Something about. . . .

"What happened?" the doctor was asking. "Johanna, what happened? Did you have a flashback? That happens sometimes after trauma. Is that what made you shake so?"

Hammering and grinding noises from outside rattled the overhead beams. The long, narrow fluorescent light fixture over the doctor's head trembled. If it falls, Jo thought dully, it will shatter on her skull and slice her head into little tiny pieces, just like the glass on Missy's door sliced my face.

The face that someone around here thinks no one should have to look at, not even me.

"Johanna?" the doctor was repeating. "What *is* it? Does your face hurt?"

No, her face didn't hurt. Being *scared* hurt.

She wasn't really sure what she was scared *of*. Maybe that someone could so easily enter her room, could so easily get into her purse. How had that happened?

Yesterday, Sunday, people had been in and

out of room 428 all day long. Some had come to see her, to bring her magazines and doughnuts from downstairs and find out how she was. Some had come to gawk, she knew that. There had been people in her room she didn't even know. She'd had to ask Nan or Evan or Reed who they were.

Anyone could have gotten into her purse, with so many people hanging out in her room. *Anyone*. Anyone could have taken her compact and glued thick, black fabric onto the glass. Anyone could have hidden the glass so that Johanna Donahue couldn't look at her own face.

"Jo?" The doctor's voice was sharper, and she was holding up a long, pointed needle. "If you don't snap out of this, I'm going to have to give you a shot and put you to bed."

That did it. No way was she going to be stuck in a bed in this infirmary with all that hammering and grinding and shouting going on outside. There might be a light fixture over her bed, and it might come crashing down from all that noise. . . .

"I'm fine," she said calmly, willing her arms and legs and body to stop their stupid shaking. They obeyed. "Yes, I guess I did have a flashback. I must have dozed off in class and that's when it happened."

The doctor looked unconvinced.

"Really," Jo persisted. "That's all it was. My face feels fine. I have to go now. Thanks for your help." Smoothly, without a hint of a tremble, she slid off the table and was amazed to find that her legs were remarkably steady as she stood.

Promising the doctor that she would let her know if she had any problems at all, Jo made her escape, out into the cold afternoon.

I *do* have problems, she thought as she hurried across campus, glad to be free of the infirmary. But my problems aren't medical, doctor, so you really can't help me with them. She ran into Evan halfway to Lester. He was frowning as he caught up with her. "I heard what happened," he said, peering down into her face. "You okay?"

She nodded. Should she tell him about the compact? He had already seen the mirrors in her room, so he wouldn't be that surprised. But . . . he might think she'd overreacted. Getting so upset . . .

"Yes, I'm fine," she answered, deciding not to tell him. She hardly knew him, after all. Why dump all her problems on him? "I have a headache, though," she added, wanting only to be safe in her room, where she could think about what had happened.

"We're still on for Friday night, right?"

Jo nodded absentmindedly. She was thinking how different campus looked in the dead of winter. Last October, the big old trees lining the walkways had exploded in a riot of wildly blazing red, purple, gold and russet. Now, their branches stretched bleakly upward, black and bare. The velvety grass that had been thick and green in September was hidden under a thin layer of yellowing snow left over from the most recent snowstorm.

Winter wasn't all that kind to the campus of Salem University.

But it was still beautiful and she wouldn't want to be anywhere else. That girl she'd heard about who had left so suddenly must have been really miserable there not to be able to wait until spring.

Spring . . . by spring, her face would be healed. "Good as new," the doctor had said.

Really?

Hard to believe just now.

Jo raised a hand to touch the bandage on her cheek.

"It *is* hurting, isn't it?" Evan asked, noticing the motion.

"No. But I'm cold. I need to get inside, where it's warm, okay? See you later."

When she reached the door to Lester, she

glanced over her shoulder. Evan was standing in the middle of the walkway, watching her.

Inside, their resident advisor, Bev, was sitting at the desk in the lobby. "Got a package for you," she said as Jo moved toward the elevator.

"A package? For me?"

"Um-hmm." Bev reached down beneath the desk and pulled out a large, octagonal-shaped box. Yellow stripes. Big yellow bow on top. But strangely, there was no card.

"Who's it from?"

Bev shrugged. "Some delivery guy dropped it off." She glanced up at Jo. "Your birthday?"

"My birthday's in July." But Jo took the box and looped the yellow ribbon over her wrist. Her mother wouldn't send a care package in this kind of box. It looked like a hatbox. Her mother never wore hats.

Besides, the box was from a local department store. Ogilvie's. Very expensive. Nan shopped there all the time.

Jo smiled. Had her friends gotten a get-well gift for her? Had Nan and Kelly hunted all over Ogilvie's for just the perfect thing to cheer her up?

What a sweet thing to do!

"Sorry about your accident," Bev said. "You okay?"

Jo nodded and headed for the elevator. The fourth floor hall was quiet. Good. Maybe she could take a quick nap before Kelly got home.

But first, she wanted to see what Nan and Kelly had selected for her.

She dropped the box on her bed, along with her books and jacket. After taking an aspirin for her headache, she returned to the bed and lifted the lid on the yellow-striped box.

Tissue paper . . . mounds of pale yellow tissue paper.

Jo unfolded the sheets of yellow to reveal what was hidden inside.

Black . . . a pile of black, lying there in the depths of the box.

And suddenly Jo knew — this was *not* a get-well gift from her friends.

Jo's hands began to shake. As if hypnotized, she reached down and withdrew the black object lying in the yellow-striped box.

It *was* a hat.

She held in her hands a wide-brimmed black hat. A thickly layered black veil hung from the brim all the way around its edges.

If I put this hat on, Jo thought numbly, holding it out in front of her, my face will disappear from sight. If I put this hat on and drop this veil over my face, I'll be just like the draped mirrors. Hidden. Not one part of my face will show.

That's what someone wants. Someone wants my face hidden. Someone wants me to put on this hat and hide my face from view.

Chapter 8

Jo was still sitting on her bed, staring down at the black hat, slowly turning it around and around in her hands, when Kelly and Nan walked in. They dropped their books on Kelly's bed and turned to face Jo.

"Where did you get *that*?" Kelly asked, coming over to take a closer look at the hat. "Is that what you're wearing to Cath's party? What are you going as, a grieving widow?"

Nan reached out playfully, grabbed the hat and plopped it on her head, letting the thick veil fall across her features. Hidden behind the layers of sheer black, she whispered loudly, "I'm a famous movie star and I vant to be alone!"

Kelly laughed, but Jo thought dispiritedly, I was right. With that veil on, Nan's face is completely hidden. Only the hat wasn't sent to Nan. It was sent to *me*.

"Jo?" Kelly asked then. "What's wrong? You look kind of . . . weird."

Exactly. Which was why she'd been given the hat.

Realizing her mistake, Kelly added quickly, "I mean, you look kind of upset. Where did you get that monstrosity?"

Jo didn't want to talk about it. But she knew Kelly wouldn't let up until she had an answer. "Someone sent it to me." She had already dug around in the box, looking for some kind of card or note that might give her a clue to the sender. But there was nothing.

Nan removed the hat, let it sail onto Jo's bed. It lay there accusingly, its veils draped over the edge of the quilt. "Someone sent you this hat? What for?"

Even more painful than receiving the hat was having to explain its presence. "Do I have to spell it out?" Jo asked heatedly. "You had it on. And while you had it on, we couldn't see your face. The hat was sent to *me*. *Now* do you get it?"

Nan got it. Her cheeks turned pink. "Oh, Jo, I'm sorry. What a stupid, mean thing to do! That's not funny at all."

"I don't think it was supposed to be funny. It wasn't intended as a joke, I'm positive. I think someone on campus is really freaked about my face." She told them about her compact mirror. "That's just not the kind of thing someone does to be funny."

Kelly nodded. "You're right. It's not. But someone with a sick sense of humor might think it was funny." She walked over to the bed and picked up the hat. Then she went to the window, yanked it open, and tossed the hat out.

"Kelly!" Nan cried, running to the window to look out, "what did you do that for? Maybe we could have used it to find out who's playing these disgusting jokes on Jo."

"Too late," Kelly said, closing the window and turning away from it. "Good riddance, I say. Jo doesn't need that awful thing lying around the room, reminding her. Look, are we going downtown or not?"

Nan's fingers had walked through the small yellow pages section of the local telephone book and found a listing for a costume shop in Twin Falls. "I've got my heart set on going as Marie Antoinette," she said, focusing her thickly lashed, turquoise eyes on Jo. Nan was a French major so Jo wasn't surprised. "If you don't feel like coming with us now, we could pick out a costume for you." She smiled. "You know we both have exquisite taste."

Jo thought for a minute. Thanks to Kelly, the hat was gone. Why not forget about it?

Brooding about it wasn't going to erase what had happened in the last couple of days. Evan was going to Cath's party, so she wanted to look as good as humanly possible.

Jo stood up. "I'm up for it. Let's go." She laughed, a sharp edge to the sound. "Maybe I can find a mask that covers me from the top of my head to my toes. Then no one could possibly be offended."

They both scolded her for her remark, insisting that she looked "fine."

Jo fought a small wave of envy, looking at her two friends. Neither of them needed a veil! They couldn't possibly understand how she felt. No one could.

Except maybe that girl who had left campus so suddenly. Someone had said her face had been badly mangled in a car wreck in the fall, that she'd returned to campus with severe scarring.

At least mine is temporary, Jo told herself. If the doctor's telling me the truth. If she isn't, I'll go out and buy my *own* hat, complete with a veil.

Nothing at the costume shop appealed to Jo. The small store was crowded, and much too hot. People were jostling each other to get to the costume they wanted, and then they had

59

to wait in line for the dressing room.

The manager, an elderly woman with bright blonde hair, seemed surprised but pleased to be so busy. "Haven't had this big a crowd since Halloween," she said as she brought more costumes out from the back of the store. "Somebody having a party?" Then, in a loud, brassy voice, she said to Jo, "My goodness, child, what on earth happened to your face?"

Jo ignored the woman's question. But she thought to herself, if Cath Devon were in the store right now I'd strangle her for doing something as dumb as planning a costume party. Cath's excuse had been that she'd been sick at Halloween and hadn't made it to any parties. Why couldn't she just wait until next October, like everybody else?

To Nan's delight, there was a Marie Antoinette costume, complete with curly white wig. Kelly settled on dressing like Morticia from the Addams Family. Jo halfheartedly tried on half a dozen costumes, but nothing seemed right, especially with her bandages.

Then the store manager came over to say, "I think I have something that would be perfect on you. Wait here." When she returned, she was carrying an armload of black.

Jo's heart sank. "I'm *not* going as a widow," she said defensively.

"No, no, this is a Catwoman costume," the heavyset woman said. "From the Batman movie? It's brand-new. A black unitard, black high-heeled boots and," she held up a satiny black object, "a mask."

Perfect! Jo flashed her a brilliant smile. "I'll try it on. Thanks."

The outfit was better than perfect. Jo didn't have an ounce of fat on her anywhere, so she looked great in the long, lean, one-piece leotard. And the mask did exactly what she needed it to do. It slipped on over her hair like a helmet, leaving only her eyes, mouth and chin visible. Great!

When she emerged from the dressing room, Nan and Kelly, their costumes already plastic-bagged, were standing by the counter at the front of the store.

"Me-oww!" Jo whispered loudly.

The two girls turned. "Jo?" Kelly's big brown eyes got bigger. "Is that you? You look fantastic!"

"*Where* did you get that?" Nan wanted to know, a touch of envy in her voice.

"Batman mailed it to me," Jo replied, twirling in front of the full-length mirror. "Isn't it great! Now, I actually feel like going to this party. All right!"

"All you need is a whip," Kelly suggested.

"I'll bet that sporting-goods store across the street has one."

As usual, Kelly knew exactly what finishing touch was needed.

"Oscar's? Would they have a whip?"

Kelly shrugged. "Why not? They have everything over there. You should at least try it."

The costume *would* be much better with a whip.

"I'm going to run over there," Jo said. "Here's some money for the rental fee. You pay for me, okay? I'll be right back." She ran back into the dressing room, changed, and hurried out of the store.

The fresh air, even though it was cold, felt wonderful. Jo waited at the corner to cross with the light. What a great costume! She wouldn't have to give a second thought to the tape on her face. No one would be able to see it, and she'd still look good. *Really* good. Too bad Evan wasn't going as Batman, but the store owner had shaken her head regretfully when Jo asked. No Batman costume.

Too bad. But then, life couldn't be *too* perfect, could it?

The light turned yellow. She was just about to cross when she spotted a tall, dark-haired figure across the street, about to enter the sporting-goods store. Evan? That looked like his leather jacket. Great! She could find out what he was wearing to Cath's party. Would he even wear a costume? Probably not.

There was no sign of Evan inside the store, or anyone else in a leather jacket. It was a big store, and Jo realized she might just be missing him. But he was tall . . . shouldn't his head show over the tops of the counters?

Maybe it hadn't been him after all. Leather jackets weren't exactly rare at Salem.

She didn't find a whip in the store. She was about to give up when she spotted, on a physical-fitness equipment rack, a shiny black jump rope with black handles. She could cut it to make it shorter. And it cost less than five dollars. Perfect!

She paid for the jump rope and, plastic bag in hand, returned to the costume shop.

Carl and Reed were there, trying to talk Evan into joining them in costume as the Marx Brothers.

So she *had* seen Evan, after all. He must have gone into one of the stores flanking the sporting goods shop. She couldn't remember what kind of stores they were.

"C'mon, Evan, we need a third," Carl argued as Evan remained staunch in his refusal to wear a costume. "We'll even let you be Groucho. Jo, *talk* to him! Use your ample charms to change his mind."

If he were talking to Nan or Kelly, he would have said *beauty*, not *charm*, Jo thought resentfully. And immediately felt ashamed. She was *not* going to let the creep who had covered her mirrors and mailed her that awful hat get to her. No way.

"If Evan chooses not to wear a costume," she said loftily, "and be totally out of it at a party where everyone else is wearing one, who am I to persuade him otherwise?"

Evan laughed. "Well, if Jo's wearing one, I suppose I could, too. We might as well both look silly."

Jo liked the way that sounded. Evan had linked them together. Nice.

Costumes in hand, they left the shop, heading for Vinnie's, a popular pizza hangout in town.

While the guys went to play a quick game of pool, Jo, Kelly, and Nan grabbed a booth. They were studying the menus when a voice said, "Well, hello there, Jo. I'm glad to see you've recovered nicely."

Jo looked up to see the doctor from the infirmary smiling down at her. "Not having any trouble, are you?" the woman, carrying a large white pizza box, asked.

"No, Doctor Trent, I'm fine." Except for some really strange things that have been happening, Jo wanted to add. "I'll be in on Friday to have the dressings checked."

"Good. See you then. Have fun." Waving, the doctor moved away.

Reed arrived back at the booth as she was leaving. "I'm no match for the pool wizards," he said, sliding in beside Kelly. He glanced toward the doorway. "Man," he said, shaking his head, "I think I feel a case of the flu coming on. If I was sure I'd get Doctor Gorgeous there, I'd concentrate on giving myself a fever."

"She *is* pretty," Kelly said grudgingly. "In a sort of brisk, efficient way."

"She's beautiful," Jo amended. "And she's really very nice. Great bedside manner."

Reed leered. "Bedside manner?"

Kelly jabbed him in the ribs with an elbow.

Seeing the doctor reminded Jo again of her wounds. She found herself glancing around the pizza parlor just as she had in the costume shop. But other than a few mildly curious glances sent her way, no one seemed to be staring at her in a way designed to make the little hairs on the back of her neck stand at attention.

Maybe the hat had been the last of the nasty pranks. Even a weirdo had to realize that certain jokes got stale pretty quick.

The others were talking about the upcoming party, about classes, and about the weather forecast, which included a warming trend. The only sour note came when Carl mentioned the ongoing search for the missing student, Sharon Westover. "It turns out she didn't go home, after all," he announced, scooping a glob of mozzarella from the last piece of pizza and depositing it in his mouth. "I heard this morning. I guess her parents are going nuts, wondering where she is."

Annoyed with Carl for bringing up such a gloomy topic, Jo quickly changed the subject. By the time they returned to their room, her head was beginning to ache again, and she suddenly felt very tired. But she'd had fun. She'd felt almost normal again.

Nan went back to her own room to study, and Kelly disappeared into the bathroom.

Jo flopped down on her bed lengthwise and switched on her bedside lamp. She wanted to take another look at the Catwoman mask. It was so perfect. . . .

Jo reached under her bed and pulled out the plastic bag from the costume store. Wait until Evan saw her in this outfit! She hoped Nan and Kelly hadn't told him what she was wearing. It would be more fun if she took him by surprise.

When Jo opened the bag, something fell out and landed on the hardwood floor with a soft plop.

The mask wouldn't make a sound like that. Besides, it was still inside the bag. She could feel it.

She hung her head over the edge of the bed to see what had fallen.

A beige, plastic tube.

Jo stared at it, frowning.

I didn't buy anything in a tube, she thought, reaching down to pick up the container.

Tube in hand, she hoisted herself up on her elbows and read the label.

BAN-BLEM.

Ban-Blem?

Jo had never heard of it. She had certainly never *bought* it.

Where had it come from?

And what *was* it?

Rolling over on her back, Jo held the tube up to the light and read the label.

A FULL-COVERAGE CORRECTIVE MAKEUP SPECIALLY FORMULATED TO COVER BIRTHMARKS, SCARS, AND BLEMISHES SO SKIN APPEARS FLAW-LESS. WATERPROOF. DERMATOLO-GIST-TESTED.

Jo dropped the tube as if it were ablaze. It rolled off the bed and fell to the floor.

Corrective makeup . . . to hide scars and blemishes . . . to make skin look flawless . . .

He — or she — had done it again.

Chapter 9

The special makeup was a stroke of genius. No mistaking that message. If Johanna can't figure out that she'd better cover up that grotesque face of hers, she's not as smart as everyone thinks she is.

My patience is running out. If she would just take the hint and hide in her room until we know if there's any permanent damage, I could let her live until the bandages come off and we see how bad it is. But oh, no, she has to play the brave soldier and face the world. She refuses to take my hints, refuses to stay hidden. Why can't she see that that's the best thing?

It worked for me, didn't it? Even when I begged to be allowed outside, cried and pleaded to join the rest of the world, They knew how disastrous it would be for me. They protected me. That was Their job, and They did it well.

That's all I'm trying to do for Jo. But she's ignoring me. I cannot tolerate this much longer. She is actually planning to go to that party at Nightmare Hall. How can she? How can anyone else have a good time if she's there? It's not fair of her to ruin the party for the rest of us.

Well, this is not the first time I've had to deal with someone so stubborn. They leave me no choice. Foolish of them.

I, too, am stubborn. And I know what I must do.

Soon . . . it must be soon. . . .

Chapter 10

Jo's mind began racing. When could someone have put that tube in her plastic bag? Had to be at Vinnie's. Where had she put the bag while she was eating? At her feet, under the table? *On* the table, at her elbow? She couldn't remember. She had left the table twice: once to go to the restroom, another time to pick out a song on the jukebox. Had she taken the bag with her? She didn't think so.

She had thought no one was paying any attention to her. She'd been wrong about that. Someone must have been watching her every move.

Jo shuddered.

Kelly, emerging from the bathroom with her hair turbanned in a white towel, caught the shudder. "Are you cold? They're getting pretty stingy with the heat lately, if you ask me."

"No, I'm not cold." Jo debated for a second,

and then reached down and picked up the tube. "I found this in my bag from Oscar's. I didn't buy it."

Kelly took the tube, read the label. She shrugged. "The clerk must have given it to you by mistake." She handed the tube back to Jo.

"Kelly, this bag is from a *sporting-goods* store. They don't carry makeup."

Kelly sat down on her bed. "They carry sunscreen, for skiers. How do you know they don't carry this stuff, too?"

"They don't. Someone *else* put that tube in my bag. Probably at Vinnie's."

A frown creased Kelly's smooth, unblemished skin. "Why?" Then her face cleared. "Oh. Is this . . . is this like the hat? Someone telling you not to go out without . . . without hiding your . . . what happened to your face?"

Jo nodded. "Looks that way. I don't care about *that*. I'm not worried about what my face looks like." That was *almost* true. "What I *hate* is the idea that someone is *watching* me. Did you see anyone at our booth when I went to the restroom or the jukebox?"

Kelly shook her turbanned head. "I don't think so. I mean, there were lots of people in and around the booth. But I don't remember noticing anyone we don't know." She got up and went to the dresser mirror to remove the towel and shake her dark hair free. "So, are you going to use it?"

"Use what?"

"That stuff. That Ban-Blem. When your bandages come off, I mean. It might help."

Hurt and angry, Jo rolled over and faced the wall.

Kelly continued blithely, "You're coming skiing with us Wednesday afternoon right? No one has classes after one o'clock, so we're going over to the state park. You can bring Evan if you want."

Jo, feigning sleep, didn't answer. Okay, so Kelly had been more polite than the person who put that tube of Ban-Blem in the bag, but wasn't her message pretty much the same one: Johanna, hide your imperfections from the public? Use the stuff in the tube, use a veil, use a mask, use whatever you have to, but please don't offend our eyes by making us look at your scars. Kelly probably didn't even know she had said that. But she *had*.

Wednesday proved to be a perfect day for skiing. Cold, but sunny and bright, with a brilliant blue winter sky overhead.

"Are you sure it's okay for you to go skiing?" Nan asked when she arrived at room 428 wearing a powder-blue ski outfit and matching visored cap. "I mean, maybe you should check with the doctor first."

"I didn't break my leg, Nan," Jo said crossly. "What does my face have to do with skiing?"

Nan shrugged. "I was just trying to be helpful, Jo. You don't need to bite my head off. What if you fall? Your bandages will get all wet."

"So? I'll put new ones on."

Nan shrugged. "I'm just trying to help. Excuse me for caring."

Jo flushed guiltily. I am really getting paranoid, she thought, apologizing to Nan.

Later that afternoon while Jo was having a mug of cocoa, Missy Stark was kind enough to inform her that the patio door had been repaired. "And my father says we'll pay your medical bills," she added stiffly. "Although personally, I think whoever pushed you should have to pay them."

"*Pushed* me?" Jo echoed. "No one pushed me. I just got swept up by the crowd."

They were in the lodge, sitting on a bench close to a roaring fire in the huge stone fireplace. Beyond the huge picture windows on one side of the room, skiers milled about on the slopes in the bright sunshine. Upbeat music filled the big, cozy room where Jo and Missy sat among the others taking a break from the wind and sun and snow.

"Are you sure?" Missy fixed narrowed eyes on Jo's bandaged face. "No one *else* fell. In that whole crowd, you were the only one who got knocked off your feet. It looked to me like someone rammed you into that door on purpose." Having said that, Missy jumped up in response to her name being called out. Reminding Jo to send any medical bills to her father, Missy left the lodge.

Jo stared into the fire. *Pushed?* Missy thought someone had deliberately pushed her through that door?

That was crazy. Who would do that? No one. No one would do that.

Missy didn't know what she was talking about. There'd been a total panic about the fire. How could Missy possibly know what had happened?

Pushed? No way.

But when Evan arrived, a cup of hot coffee in his hand, Jo told him about Missy's disturbing theory.

"She thinks someone pushed you?" He sipped his coffee thoughtfully. "So, is that a possibility? You made someone at the party mad? Maybe a jealous boyfriend who freaked when he saw you falling into my clutches?"

Jo shook her head. "No. I didn't start making people mad at me until *after* I went through the door."

Evan didn't laugh. "So you don't think you were pushed?"

"Only by the crowd. Couldn't be helped."

"You're sure?"

Was she? Jo struggled to remember. True, the crowd had been pressing in on her, forcing her feet forward. But . . . hadn't she felt something in the small of her back, something that wasn't just the vague pressure of a mass of bodies?

A . . . hand?

It could have been a hand reaching out for support . . . someone afraid they were about to fall. "Yes," she said with as much certainty as she could manage, "I'm sure."

Because with everything else that had happened, she simply couldn't allow herself to believe that someone at that party, someone she *knew*, had deliberately shoved her into that glass door. That was just too scary.

Anyone who might have done such a thing would have to have known she'd be hurt. Seriously hurt. Even . . . killed. Dr. Trent had said in the infirmary that night, "Another quarter-inch to the left and this chunk of glass in your neck would have hit the carotid artery. You're a very lucky girl."

She didn't have any enemies like that.

Did she?

Carl and Reed, Kelly and Nan joined them at the fireplace then, bringing with them harmless, casual conversation. Other students arrived, among them several people with obvious sun and wind burns. A tall, thin, dark-haired girl from Jo's English class had cheeks as red as her parka, and her lips were already spotted with white, the beginnings of some serious blistering. Her name was Tina Downs. She was friendly, and funny. Jo had always liked her.

"Oh," Tina moaned as she sat down on the floor, "I stayed out there too long. I left the Quad with no sunscreen. I should have come in here every time you did, Jo. Why didn't you *drag* me out of that sun?"

"You wouldn't have gone," a blond-haired boy sitting beside her said. "You were too busy showing off. Although," he added admiringly, "you *are* pretty good. Care to give me a few lessons?"

"In what?" Tina asked, although she was clearly finding it difficult to talk. She groaned again. "I know I'm blistering, I can feel it. I'm going to show up at Cath's party Friday night looking like I was staked out in a desert!"

Looking at Tina's blistering lips, Jo was grateful that she'd put sunscreen on the parts of her face that weren't covered with bandages. A sunburn like that must be really painful. She didn't need *that* right now.

Tina Downs wouldn't be getting a lot of sleep tonight.

"You really ought to stop in the infirmary when you get back, Tina," Jo said. "They might be able to give you something so you won't be so miserable. Your lips are blistering fast."

Clearly already miserable, Tina nodded. "Maybe I will."

They all stopped at Burgers Etc. on the way home. Then the combination of fresh air and exercise hit them and they piled into their cars and headed back to campus.

As she crawled into bed that night, Jo rejoiced. She had gone skiing, and nothing terrible had happened. No nasty messages hidden in her ski jacket's pockets, or in her shoulderbag, no packages delivered to the lodge or the ski slope, and no staring or whispering. She was old news now. Everyone was used to her bandages.

She hadn't even fallen.

Not a bad day, she thought, letting sleep overtake her. Not a bad day at all. Maybe it's all over now. The person who made it his mission in life to make me as miserable as possible probably got tired of the game. Or ran out of ideas.

About time.

Hoping he hadn't picked some other innocent victim to target, Jo drifted off to sleep.

Chapter 11

Well, this is just great! Now I've got two of them to deal with! Sometimes it just gets to be too much.

Tina Downs is an idiot. Who goes skiing on a day like this without sunscreen? I could hardly stand looking at her. Those disgusting blisters. I thought she'd never leave Burgers so I could eat in peace. And I was starving.

I have decided to let her live, in spite of her stupidity. Her blisters, ugly though they are, are temporary.

But Johanna's scars will be permanent. I must forget about Downs, who will recover, and concentrate on Jo, who won't.

I just hope I don't run into Downs before those blisters heal. I might not be able to control myself. Sometimes I don't seem to have total control. Probably because I take my responsibilities so seriously.

I know They would be so proud of me, if They knew.

One day, I'll tell Them.

I can't wait to see the looks on Their faces.

Now, about that party at Nightmare Hall. . . .

Chapter 12

The day of the party at Nightmare Hall arrived without incident. There were no more packages, no more "stunts" designed to intimidate Jo into hiding her face from the public.

I was right, she thought, *whoever it was finally tired of the game.*

She tried on the Catwoman mask more than once, adjusting the thin, lightweight latex around her tape and bandages. The real problem was her thick, curly hair. There was too much of it. But after several attempts, she managed to stuff it up under the helmet-like mask so that not a single auburn strand showed.

On the afternoon of the party, she stopped in at the infirmary to have her stitches checked. The racket from the construction outside was deafening. "Are they ever going to finish that wall?" she asked Dr. Trent as the doctor inspected her needlework.

Dr. Trent shook her head. "Who knows? The ground started to freeze up on them sooner than they'd expected, and that put them behind schedule. I've taken to wearing earplugs when I'm not with a patient, to save my hearing."

She declared the stitches to be in fine shape and promised to take them out early the following week. "Until then, just keep them dry, okay, Jo?"

Nodding, Jo slipped into her copper-colored suede jacket. "Am I going to have a scar?"

"Umm, maybe a tiny one." The doctor smiled. "Just enough to give your beautiful face an exotic touch. Nothing to worry about."

Satisfied with that, Jo left the infirmary.

A few hours later, Lester dorm was chaotic. Cath's party, unlike Missy's, was not open. But Nightmare Hall was big enough to hold a lot of people, and many Lester residents had been invited. They were all trying to get ready at the same time.

Nan almost got stuck in the doorway of room 428 when she arrived to see how Jo and Kelly were doing. She had to move sideways so the huge pink skirt of her gown could be stuffed through the opening. The maneuver tilted her elaborate white wig to one side. "How are you going to dance in that outfit?" Jo asked, laughing, as Nan adjusted her wig. "You look like a wedding cake!" But her laughter hid a pang of envy. Nan looked so beautiful as Marie Antoinette. The white curled wig brought out the turquoise in her eyes and the flawlessness of her skin. Kelly, too, looked stunning as Morticia, in a slinky black dress, her black wig long and sleek, her huge, dark eyes carefully outlined with black pencil.

Nan shrugged bare shoulders. "I'll manage. You look fantastic," she added generously, taking in Jo's shiny black outfit.

"So do you," Jo said, ashamed of her crack about the wedding cake. "Help me with this helmet, will you?"

Nan helped her stuff the curly mass up underneath Jo's head covering and gently eased the thin latex down over the tape and bandages.

Then she stood back and aimed a critical eye at Jo. "Perfect!" Nan announced. But the look in Evan's eyes when he arrived told her all she needed to know about her costume.

Nightmare Hall looked a lot less gloomy than usual with bright light shining from every window. Cars lined the upwardly curving driveway and music and laughter rang out from within.

"They should have a party here every night," Carl said as they all piled out of his convertible. "Makes this monstrosity look almost welcoming."

Jo and Evan were the only two who had never been inside Nightmare Hall. She was eager to see what it was like. "I love old houses," she confided to Evan, dressed as Groucho Marx, complete with thick black mustache and fake cigar as he took her hand and led her up the wide stone steps.

"You do?" He seemed surprised. "Not me. I grew up in one. No matter how much money my parents poured into it, it never looked new or perfect."

Jo laughed. "They're not *supposed* to look new, Evan. That's part of their charm. And I can't wait to see this one. I'll bet it has all kinds of secret nooks and crannies."

Cath Devon, dressed as Glinda the Good Witch from *The Wizard of Oz*, complete with star-studded wand, met them at the door. "Jo? Is that you?" She let them all into a huge foyer crowded with people. Most were costumed. Only a handful of people in regular clothes sat on the wide, curving stairs. "You look wonderful!"

Before Evan would let her check out the house, he insisted they dance. The huge library on the first floor had been cleared of furniture, and the music coming from there was slow and mellow. "Okay, one dance," Jo agreed. "Then I want to explore, okay?"

The big, book-lined room was romantically lit with candlelight, Jo's favorite song was playing, and although the room was full of other dancers, it wasn't overcrowded. Not like at Missy's.

Jo relaxed and let the music melt her bones.

I am, she thought firmly as she nestled her head against Evan's shoulder, going to have a wonderful time tonight. If anyone tries to spoil it for me, I'll give them thirty lashes with my jump rope.

"You look fantastic in that getup," Evan said. "Where'd you get the whip?"

"At Oscar's. Across the street from the costume shop." She lifted her head to look up at him. "I thought I saw you going in there, too. The day we found the costumes?"

He shook his head. "Not me. I was going next door, but they didn't have what I wanted, so I just hiked on over to the costume shop."

She would have asked him what was next door to Oscar's, but just then, she spotted another sleek black outfit leaving the room.

"Oh, no," she cried in dismay. "Another Cat-woman?"

The music stopped and Kelly, who was standing with Reed behind Jo and Evan said, "Relax, Jo. That's Tina Downs. But she's not Catwoman, she's a cat *burglar*. You know, black stirrup pants, black turtleneck sweater and gloves, black boots and a black ski mask. Her face is peeling and she wanted to hide it. But she must be so hot and uncomfortable in that outfit. Can you imagine wearing wool over a face that's peeling from sunburn? Gross!"

"Well, I know how she feels," Jo said. "My mask is tugging at my tape. I'm tempted to find a bathroom and take the bandages off, just for tonight."

"Oh, don't do that," Kelly cried impulsively.

"Not a good idea," Reed agreed.

Even Evan said, "Didn't the doctor say you should keep your cuts covered?"

Jo stared at them. "I wasn't," she said coolly, "going to run around the party with my scarred face hanging out. I planned to keep the mask *on*."

"We didn't mean that," Evan said, aware that Jo was hurt. "We just — "

"Yeah, you just," Jo said heatedly. And she turned and hurried out of the room.

Evan called after her, but she kept going.

Were they so terrified of seeing what her face looked like without tape or bandages hiding the cuts?

Well, aren't *you*? she asked herself. Aren't you scared to death to see what you're going to look like when your skin sees the light of day again? You haven't even peeked under the tape, not once. Why is that, Johanna?

That's different, she thought as she began climbing the wide, curving stairs. It's *my* face. I'm allowed to be worried about it. But my friends should like me for myself and not be so afraid of what I'm going to look like. It shouldn't make any difference to them.

Jo kept going until she reached the top of the house. Maybe by the time she went back down to the first floor, she'd be over her irritation with her friends.

The attic smelled wonderful . . . a combination of cedar and mothballs and old clothes. Although it seemed like a great place to hide, Jo was already beginning to regret her anger. The memory of her dance with Evan tugged at her. If she went back downstairs, she might get another dance or two before the night was over.

Why ruin a perfectly good party by being stubborn?

Giving the cozy room under the eaves a last

fond look, Jo went back downstairs.

But before she could look for Evan, Cath, hurrying back and forth between the kitchen and the library and living room, asked if Jo could help her out for a minute. "I need soda. It's in the cellar. Could you run down and bring up a couple of those big plastic bottles?"

She followed Cath into the kitchen. "Is it dark down there?" Jo asked hesitantly.

"No, the light's on. Just be careful going down the stairs in those high-heeled boots, okay? I don't want you falling again. And leave the door all the way open so it won't swing shut."

Jo hesitated at the top of the stairs. There *was* a light on down there, but its glow didn't reach as far as the stairs. The light from the kitchen only spread halfway down, leaving the bottom half dozen steps in darkness.

Cath hefted a large party tray and aimed for the living room. "Just set the soda in the fridge, okay? Thanks, Jo."

Jo made her way down the stairs very carefully. She had no intention of falling at *this* party. She was a little nervous when she reached the lower stairs and had to feel with her hand along the wooden railing and explore with her feet to find her footing.

But once in the cellar itself, there was a faint

yellow glow from a lone bulb hanging near the huge black, noisy furnace.

She hadn't expected the cellar to be so cold. The furnace heat was being dispatched up into the house and did little to warm the earthen-floored, gray, stone-walled space. One tiny window was set high into a far wall. There were shelves loaded with tools, and other shelves full of canned goods and glass jars. At the end near the window, boxes and trunks and suitcases were piled high.

The entire space smelled musty.

Jo wondered if there were spiders.

Shivering, Jo hurried over to an old wooden table along one wall. It was loaded with soda bottles and cans. Filling her arms, she turned and headed through the chill to the stairs.

She had just put one booted foot on the bottom step when she heard a noise above her.

She raised her head. "Evan?"

But it wasn't Evan at the top of the stairs. Above her, the kitchen was dark. Hadn't she left the kitchen light on? Cath wouldn't have turned it off, would she?

The cellar light didn't reach to the top of the stairs. All Jo could see was a shadowy figure outlined above her. It could be anyone. But if it wasn't Evan staring down at her, who *was* it?

Lost in shadow, the top of the stairs suddenly seemed miles away. Jo peered upward, trying to make out the identity of the person who seemed to be staring down at her. "Who's that?" she called. "Who's up there?"

The vague, dark figure at the top of the stairs lifted a foot, as if to begin moving downward to join her.

And then Jo thought she saw a second shadowy figure outline appear behind the first.

She heard the first figure utter a surprised grunt.

Then she saw it pitch forward, arms flying out as if to grab something, anything, to stop the fall that was coming. It made a sound, a startled cry for help.

The figure plummeted downward, free-falling through the air, straight at Jo.

Before she could jump out of the way, the cellar was plunged into sudden, complete darkness, and the door at the top of the stairs slammed shut.

Jo opened her mouth to scream, but no sound came out.

Then it was too late. Something warm and heavy slammed into her chest, knocking her off her feet, propelling her backward into the stone wall behind her. There was a sharp crack as the human missile collided, headfirst, with the wall. The figure went limp, a dead weight lying half on, half off a stunned and horrified Jo, who was sitting with her back against the wall, her legs straight out in front of her.

Shaking her head to clear it, Jo gently, gingerly, pushed against the dead weight imprisoning her. She managed to free herself enough to slide out from beneath the heavy burden.

But she could see nothing.

She sat there on the cold, damp earthen floor, trying to think. Help. . . . she had to get help. She had to get help. Someone had been hurt. Someone had fallen . . . been pushed . . . fallen . . . and was hurt. Needed . . . help.

Before she could stir her paralyzed limbs into action, the door upstairs suddenly flew open and the light came on again.

Jo blinked. Tried to lift her head to look up. Her neck hurt. Couldn't lift it.

"Jo? Jo!"

Evan's voice.

"Oh," was all she could say. "Oh."

"What . . . ?" Evan ran down the stairs, landing at the bottom to crouch at Jo's side. "Jo? What happened?"

Jo turned her head slightly to stare at the figure lying so lifelessly beside her, its arms and legs splayed out around it.

Black . . . black arms, black legs, black mask . . .

There were only two people at Cath Devon's party dressed completely in black. One was Johanna Donahue. The other was Tina Downs.

"Tina?" Jo asked tentatively, crawling over to kneel beside the frighteningly still girl. "Tina?"

Tina didn't answer.

Chapter 13

Evan felt for Tina's pulse.

"Is she alive?" Jo asked anxiously. "Is Tina alive?"

"Are you okay?" he asked. "What are you doing down here?"

Jo was too dazed to think clearly. What *was* she doing in the cellar? "I don't know. Cath wanted something, I think . . . is Tina dead?"

"No. She's alive. Must have hit her head. And it looks like she might have a broken leg, too."

"There was this terrible sound when she hit." Jo shuddered. "Are you sure she's not dead?"

"She's not dead. But we need an ambulance, fast. Can you go up and call one?"

"I'm not sure my legs will work. But I'll try."

She stepped in something when she got to the top step, and nearly fell. She grabbed the handrail just in time. Something . . . something slippery . . . on the top step. . . .

She called the ambulance, and then alerted Cath that something terrible had happened.

The word spread quickly. Curious party guests began to fill the kitchen, piling up in the cellar doorway, murmuring as they watched.

When the ambulance had come and gone, Evan turned to Jo in the kitchen and said solemnly, "I thought it was you lying down there. I'd been looking all over for you. Couldn't find you anywhere. The cellar was the only place I hadn't looked, so I decided I might as well try there, too. It was so dark though, I couldn't see much. Could barely make out a figure in black, lying there like she was dead. I thought it was you, thought that was why I couldn't find you, because you'd fallen and were hurt."

"Oh, Evan."

"Then I turned the cellar light on, and saw you sitting there." His voice strengthened, became normal. "What happened, anyway? You said she was pushed?"

"I . . . I'm not sure. I thought I saw someone, but there's a puddle on the top step. She might have slipped on it and fallen."

"I guess I missed it. I took the steps two at a time. Show me where."

Jo led Evan to the staircase and pointed.

The top step was clean. No wet puddle there.

"What are you guys looking at?" Kelly asked as she came into the kitchen. Her face was very pale.

Jo turned. "There was something spilled on this step. Now it's gone."

"Oh, that. I think it was soda. I wiped it off before the paramedics got here. I was afraid they'd fall." Jo had to admit that was sensible. Still, she had wanted another look at the spill. She had so many questions, and had hoped the mess on the top step might provide an answer.

Cath came in then, and asked what they were talking about.

When Jo explained, Cath said, "There wasn't anything on that step when I left the kitchen. Jo had just gone down to the cellar. And it was just a few minutes later that Tina fell. If something was on the step, she must have spilled it herself."

Evan shook his head. "If she'd been drinking something, her cup would have fallen with her. I didn't see one down there. Besides, think about it. If she'd been standing there, looking down into the cellar, and she'd spilled something, she wouldn't have stepped in it."

"Unless she didn't *know* she'd spilled," Jo said.

"True. But then I repeat my original question: if she was drinking something, where is the cup or glass she was using?" To double-check, Evan went back down into the cellar and looked around. He found no cup or glass.

When he came back upstairs, shrugging, Kelly said impatiently, "Look, we don't know what happened. No one saw anything. Except Jo, and she doesn't really know *what* she saw. We'll just have to wait until Tina's okay. Then she can tell us if she was pushed."

She had a point. Jo nodded reluctantly. "Kelly's right. And can we get out of this kitchen now?" she added, shivering. "I keep looking down into the cellar. It's giving me the creeps."

They went into the living room, where the hushed group of party guests had gathered.

"Is somebody trying to tell us something?" said Missy Stark, dressed as Madonna. "Like, we're partying too much? I mean," she added, "two horrible accidents so close together seems a really weird coincidence to me. I think I'm staying in my room for the rest of the semester. So don't anyone invite me anywhere. I won't go."

The party broke up quickly then.

Jo decided against going to the hospital. "Tina's friends will be there. That's enough of a crowd. We'll call later to see how she's doing." As anxious as she was to hear Tina say she had not been deliberately pushed down those stairs, Jo couldn't stand the thought of hanging around a hospital. Not tonight. It would remind her too much of her own accident.

As Evan helped Jo with her coat, she struggled to make sense of what had happened. She had been warned away from this party. She'd received all kinds of messages that clearly told her she shouldn't be going out in public until her face was healed. She'd ignored them and come to the party, anyway. She *had* covered her injured face, but she'd come.

Maybe that had made someone angry.

But it was *Tina* who had flown down that flight of stairs.

As they left Nightmare Hall, Jo remembered Missy's statement at the ski lodge hinting that Jo had been deliberately pushed into that door at the Stark party.

But it wasn't *true*. She was sure of it. She'd thought about it, long and carefully. And she was still positive it had been an accident.

Just as Tina's fall had been an accident. That sticky stuff on the top step . . . anyone could have slipped on that and fallen. I almost slipped on it myself, Jo thought.

It was true that two accidents in a row was pretty weird. But stranger things had happened, right?

Some vague, unformed thought tugged at the back of Jo's consciousness . . . something that made her uneasy . . . something she couldn't identify. What *was* it?

She was too tired to wrestle with it now. Later . . .

Kelly, Nan, Carl and Reed decided to go to Vinnie's, but Jo had lost her appetite. She insisted that Evan drop her off back on campus.

"You don't have to walk me in," she said. "Go on to Vinnie's with them."

"I don't want to go to Vinnie's with them." He closed the car door and grabbed her hand. "What's wrong?"

"Nothing." Liar. She began walking across the Commons, huddling in her suede jacket for warmth. The mask was irritating her face, pulling at her bandages. She couldn't wait to get it off. Such a great costume . . . but such a bad night, after all.

"At first I thought Tina's fall was an accident," Evan said. "But I'm not really sure. I know *you* want to believe that. I do, too, but I can't." They were almost to Lester. It looked warm and welcoming, lights peeking from many windows, dotting the old snow with streaks of yellow. "I'm just not sure, Jo."

"It *was* an accident! Quit trying to scare me."

"Jo!" He sounded honestly appalled. "I

wasn't trying to scare you." He yanked on her hand, forcing her to stop. Then he pulled her around to face him. "It's just that when I looked down into that cellar and thought I saw you lying there . . ." He stopped. He reached out, grabbed her by the shoulders, pulled her close and kissed her.

Afterward, she leaned against him, her head on his shoulder, and said quietly, "Evan, it *wasn't* me. I'm fine. I'm just fine."

"I know."

He kissed her again at the door to her room. "You're sure you're going to be okay? Want me to stay?"

She shook her head. She wouldn't mind being alone for a while. There were things to think about.

The first thing she did after she locked the door was carefully pull the black latex mask off her face and head.

She'd been right about her hair. It was squashed flatter than a pancake. But the relief of having the rubber off her face was wonderful.

When she had changed into a long nightshirt and her robe, she sat on the bed, thinking about the party.

Jo curled her legs up underneath her and leaned back against the wall. What if Tina's fall wasn't an accident? If that were true . . . then there was something else to think about. From the back, in that darkened kitchen, all anyone would have seen was a tall, thin figure dressed head to toe in black. Tina. But . . . the figure could as easily have been Johanna Donahue. From the back, in that tiny bit of light from the cellar, the two figures could have been interchangeable.

Curling her fists into small, tight balls, Jo thought about the draped mirrors, the missing compact mirror, the hat with the veil, the cover-up cream.

"I was being warned," she murmured, her fists clenching and unclenching nervously. "I was being told to hide my face, not to show it in public. And I didn't listen. I went to the party, anyway."

Could that have made someone angry enough to . . . punish her? Punish her for not listening? For ignoring the warnings? Punish her by pushing her down a flight of stairs?

I don't know anyone like that, Jo argued with herself. I *don't*!

You mean, a little voice in the back of her head admonished, that you don't *want* to know anyone like that. But isn't it obvious that you *do*? Because if someone *did* push Tina down those stairs, they were attending the same party you were. So you *know* them. Whether you want to or not.

Had the push been meant for her instead of Tina? Who knew she was dressed as Cat-woman?

Everyone. Everyone at the party knew. She hadn't made any secret of who she was.

Her head beginning to ache, Jo lay down on the bed, pulling her comforter up over her. So many questions, but only two were important: *Had* Tina been deliberately pushed down those stairs? And if she had, had she been mistaken for Jo Donahue?

One thing was clear: if she was the one who was supposed to have fallen, then she would be stupid not to be afraid.

She wasn't stupid.

So . . . was she afraid?

Yes.

She was scared to death.

Chapter 14

Jo awoke the next morning with a headache. She took an aspirin and called the hospital to find out about Tina.

The nurse would tell her only that Tina Downs was in "fair condition."

Oh, thanks a lot, Jo thought as she hung up the phone. That tells me next to nothing.

But at least Tina was alive.

Jo glanced out the window. They'd planned to return their costumes this morning. The sun was shining brightly and the sky was cloudless. Looked like a beautiful day — maybe her mood would improve.

By the time she had showered and dressed, Kelly was awake. She asked about Tina right away.

Jo shrugged. "Fair condition, whatever that means."

"I think it means she's going to be okay. If

she weren't, she'd be in 'critical' or 'serious' condition," Kelly said. "So, what are our plans on this beautiful Saturday?"

Jo had awakened to find the stitches on her cheek bothering her, probably a result of wearing the mask the night before. They still hurt, and she found herself resenting the fact that Kelly, who hadn't been awake more than a minute, looked perfectly gorgeous.

Life just wasn't fair. "I don't *have* any plans," Jo said irritably. "Except, we have to return our costumes."

"Are the guys going with us?"

And then, for no other reason than the fact that Kelly Benedict looked far more beautiful than anyone had a right to look first thing in the morning, Jo snapped, "Can't you go *anywhere* without a male by your side?"

"Hey!" Kelly sat up in bed. "Ease up. What's your problem, anyway?"

Chagrined, Jo apologized. It wasn't Kelly's fault she looked the way she did. And not her fault that Jo had gone through that glass door. She hadn't even been *in* that crowd at Missy's party. "I'm sorry. Guess I got up on the wrong side of the bed. And yes, as far as I know, they're meeting us down at the fountain at ten."

Kelly glanced at her alarm clock. "Ten?

That's only an hour away!" She threw the covers aside and jumped out of bed. Running for the bathroom, she called over her shoulder, "I'll never be ready in time, no way!"

Jo's irritation melted. It was Saturday, it was gorgeous, Evan had kissed her last night, and she was going to see him again in an hour. Best of all, Tina was not in "critical" or "serious" condition; she was in "fair" condition. Maybe she'd even be up to a telephone conversation later today.

Vowing to call the hospital when they returned from town, Jo got dressed.

They were coming out of the costume shop in Twin Falls when she glanced across the street and noticed that the sporting-goods shop was flanked by a beauty supply shop on one side and a drugstore on the other.

Beauty supplies?

Evan must have been going into the drugstore the day they rented their costumes. What would he be doing in a beauty supply store? Jo smiled to herself. Evan certainly didn't need any beauty supplies. He looked just fine the way he was.

Suddenly, without warning, a vision of the little beige tube danced before her eyes. Ban-Blem. A special corrective makeup for scars and blemishes. . . .

Wouldn't you buy that at a beauty supply store?

She was instantly ashamed. Evan? Buying a tube of makeup and hiding it in her bag from the sporting-goods store?

Never! He would never do anything so mean.

Why *would* he?

He had gone into the drugstore that day. Absolutely.

She could *ask* him. But then he'd want to know why she was so curious. Maybe he'd even figure out that she was asking because of the Ban-Blem, and he'd be furious that she could think he'd pull such a rotten stunt.

Jo tried valiantly to put the whole nasty business out of her mind. It *hadn't* been Evan. Couldn't have been.

But she found herself watching him later, at Burgers Etc., while they were eating lunch. And then, because she couldn't bear the thought that it might have been him, she found herself watching all of her friends. Reed and Carl, both so great-looking, so funny, so popular, calling out cheerfully to friends who entered the long, silver diner. Nan and Kelly, the perfect foils for Reed and Carl, with their own flawless good looks, their self-confidence, their ability to wear clothes as if the designer had had them in mind all along.

Perfect teeth, Jo found herself thinking . . . my friends all have perfect teeth. Look at all that shiny white enamel. Incredible!

And it occurred to her then that she'd been thinking far too much about looks lately. I never did that before, she thought, a little bit stunned. What's *wrong* with me?

"What's the matter with you?" Evan asked suddenly, yanking Jo out of herself.

For a second, she thought she'd spoken aloud. And quickly realized he wasn't referring to her sudden preoccupation with looks. He was talking about how quiet she'd been since they'd come from town.

"Sorry. I guess I'm still a little off-balance from last night."

"Yeah. Well, I heard Tina's going to be okay." Evan smiled. "That should make you feel better."

Jo nodded. "It does. I'm going to call her later."

"You are?" They got up then and left the diner. "What for?" Evan asked as he opened the door. "I didn't know you knew her that well."

Jo slipped red leather gloves on her hands. "I know her well enough to want to find out if she was pushed down those stairs. I thought you'd want me to find out."

They had decided to walk back to school. It wasn't that far, and it would give them some time alone. "I do," Evan answered as they crossed the highway. "But she's only been in the hospital since last night. I figured you'd wait a while, that's all."

"No time like the present," Jo quipped lightly. "But first, I have to stop off at the infirmary and talk to Dr. Trent. My stitches are driving me nuts."

"You're not going to have her take them out already, are you?" Evan sounded alarmed.

"No. But maybe she can give me something to stop the itching."

"Want some company?"

Jo shook her head. She hated the way she was feeling, wondering about Evan and the beauty supply shop, but she couldn't help it. She didn't really know him all that well, did she? He hadn't *seemed* put off by her damaged face, but maybe that was just an act. Someone who liked only new and perfect houses might like only new and perfect faces, as well.

Until she was sure of Evan, maybe she shouldn't spend a lot of time alone with him.

Telling him she'd see him later, she hurried

off toward the infirmary. She glanced over her shoulder only once.

He was still standing there, watching her go. She thought he looked puzzled.

No wonder. Last night, they'd been getting along so well. And now here she was, the very next day, acting like she'd rather have someone poking at her stitches than spend time with Evan. He must be very confused.

Join the club, Jo thought, and yanked the infirmary door open.

When Dr. Trent had checked the stitches, announced that they were a "little inflamed" and given Jo a small tube of ointment, Jo slid off the examination table and said casually, "Dr. Trent, did you know that girl who disappeared? Sharon Westover? The freshman the police have been asking about?"

Dr. Trent nodded. "Yes, I knew her. She had a lot of problems after she came back to campus following her accident. The incisions on her face weren't healing properly. I saw quite a bit of her. She was horribly depressed. Can't say that I blame her. She'd been a very pretty girl."

"Couldn't she have plastic surgery?"

"Oh, of course. But there's only so much they can do, Jo. Her face was badly crushed. Most of her facial bones were shattered. And the major reconstructive work couldn't be done right away. She wasn't handling the wait very well."

Saddened, Jo fell silent.

"I'm not surprised that she left campus," the doctor continued as she returned supplies to a cabinet over the sink. "It was hard for her. She was homecoming queen at her high school, I understand. The change in her appearance was probably impossible for her to bear. Many people your age who sustain facial injuries retreat to their rooms and never come back out." Dr. Trent smiled. "I think you've handled your injuries remarkably well, Jo. And your reward will be that you'll look good as new when your stitches come out."

That thought comforted Jo as she left the infirmary. Maybe she *was* handling her injuries well. But maybe that was because she'd been told from the beginning that there would be no permanent damage. If she'd been given the same verdict that Sharon Westover must have been given, she probably would have reacted pretty much the same way. Wanting to hide from curious or pitying or even repulsed eyes.

The construction site was silent. The crew left early on Saturdays. Because there were no workers there to observe her, Jo decided to take a walk along the riverbank instead of going directly back to Lester. There'd still be time to call Tina when she returned.

We take our looks for granted, she thought, hiking along the dirt path beside the river, now overcoated with a thick layer of ice. All of us . . . we get up in the morning and comb our hair and wash our faces and when we look in the mirror we never think how lucky we are. We never even thought very much about Sharon when we heard about the accident. We said things like, "Isn't that awful?" and "poor Sharon," but none of us thought to go see her when she came back to campus. Okay, so we didn't really know her. But we still could have welcomed her back. Showed her that she'd be okay.

Maybe we didn't *want* to see her. Maybe we were afraid, secretly, that if we saw her, we'd realize the same thing could happen to us.

It was colder out than Jo had expected, in spite of the bright sunshine. And the river wasn't nearly as interesting now that it was frozen solid under a thick sheet of snow-covered ice.

She turned around to retrace her steps to campus.

A noise behind her made her turn her head.

Nothing there.

Still, realizing how far from campus she'd

come, she instinctively hurried her steps.

And clearly heard footsteps behind her, padding softly.

She stopped, turned around.

Nothing behind her but bushes on both sides of the path, and huge old willow trees lining the riverbank.

But she was positive she'd heard footsteps.

Paranoid, she told herself with some disgust. You're getting positively paranoid. Even if there is someone back there, it's the middle of the afternoon. It's broad daylight. What can happen in broad daylight? It's probably someone out for a nice, healthy Saturday afternoon jog.

Nevertheless, she decided to break into a nice, healthy jog herself.

Instantly, the footsteps followed suit. Closer . . . they were getting closer.

But when she glanced over her shoulder a third time, the sound stopped. There was no sign of anyone in jogging sweats running along the path behind her.

If someone were out for a nice, innocent jog, they wouldn't stop running each time she did, would they? And they certainly wouldn't hide. They'd keep going, catch up with her, and pass her by.

Why were the footsteps stopping each time

she did? And why was no one there when she looked?

Taking a deep breath, Jo broke into a run.

Immediately, the feet behind her did the same. Heavy pounding on the path signaled someone running as fast as she was. Maybe faster. Running . . . after *her*?

Jo ran hard, but her heavy boots and jacket weighed her down. Her breathing became erratic, her chest began aching with the effort, but she never slowed down or paused on the path.

The steps behind her became louder. The person was closing in on her.

Broad daylight . . . it was the middle of the afternoon! Why was someone chasing her behind campus in the middle of the afternoon?

There . . . just ahead . . . Butler Hall, the big, stone administration building. There might be people there . . . someone to help her. . . .

The footsteps were just behind her, and to her horror, she could hear heavy breathing close at hand. Not labored, like hers. She was exhausted, but her pursuer wasn't.

A few more steps . . . keep going . . . don't stop now . . . almost there. . . .

The arm came out of nowhere. It wrapped

itself around Jo's neck from behind and a voice cried hoarsely, "Gotcha!"

As her feet were lifted off the ground, something black and slippery was thrown over her head. She couldn't see. The slick, slippery material melded itself to her nose and mouth. She smelled plastic . . . like . . . garbage bag plastic. . . .

One hand remained around her neck while another wrapped itself around her chest, pinning her arms to her sides. She was helpless.

Each time she breathed in, the thick black plastic plastered itself against her nose and mouth like wallpaper. Fighting panic, she whooshed air from her mouth to push away the oily, suffocating gag.

Struggling to free her arms, she opened her mouth to scream, but the intake of breath pulled the plastic back into her mouth. She spit it out and tried again. The same thing happened.

Afraid of suffocating, she gave up the attempt to scream. But she continued to kick out with her feet and wrestle to free her arms. In vain. Her attacker retained a firm grip around her neck.

"You didn't put a bag over your head the way you should have," the voice whispered in her ear, "so," chuckling, "I'm doing it for you. Isn't that nice of me?"

Rough fingers fumbled at her throat. The plastic over her head was drawn so tightly down over her face it was pressed up against her mouth and nose, and this time she couldn't blow it away. It was being held there while something . . . something was being wound around her neck. She could feel it. A rope? String? She felt it circling once, twice, then being pulled so tightly, it cut into her neck.

She couldn't breathe. And she couldn't get her arms free to yank at the plastic over her mouth and nose.

Suddenly, the arm around her chest fell away. Her arms were free. Immediately, she began flailing out wildly, her fists clenched, as rough fingers fumbled at the back of her head. Tying something . . . he was tying the black plastic around her neck. That's why he'd had to let go of her arms. He couldn't make a knot with one hand.

Each breath she drew sucked the plastic into her nostrils. And her searching fists met only air. He was behind her. How could she hit him when he was behind her?

Desperate, Jo kicked out with her legs. She connected once, twice. Her attacker yelped. But the efforts to tie the rope around her neck continued. She could feel it being knotted into place.

Then she heard crazy, frenzied laughter and the sound of footsteps running away.

Silence.

She was alone.

She was on the river path behind Butler Hall, alone with a plastic bag tied tightly around her head and neck.

And she couldn't breathe.

Chapter 15

Jo stood in the middle of the path, gasping for breath, clawing at the cord that held the black plastic firmly in place.

It was tied too tightly. Her fingers fumbled desperately to loosen the knot. And failed.

Blowing against the plastic to force it away from her mouth and nose, Jo staggered forward, pulling, tugging, on the knot at the back of her neck. Afraid that, blinded as she was, she might misstep and find herself out on the river's ice, she took only tiny steps forward.

Small blue and orange dots began to dance before her eyes.

Calm down, she warned herself sharply. If you panic, you'll hyperventilate . . . then you'll pass out . . . you're way out here behind Butler Hall . . . by the time someone finds you, you'll be long dead and frozen solid like the ice on the river. Calm down, Jo, calm down.

Continuing to puff against the plastic to keep it away from her mouth and nose, Jo gave up on the knot and focused instead on digging her fingernails into the plastic over her face. Twice, she misjudged and accidentally dug into the cuts on her face, crying out in pain.

But she kept trying.

Her efforts were futile. The plastic was tough, and wouldn't give.

If only she had something sharp . . . a knife, a nail file.

She had nothing.

Something sharp . . . *teeth* were sharp, weren't they?

Desperate for air, Jo drew in a breath, deliberately pulling the plastic into her mouth. Then she bit down on it, hard. When she had a firm grip, she ground her teeth together as hard as she could. Her jaw ached with the effort, and she gagged on the oily black slickness in her mouth.

But she kept chewing until she heard a faint ripping sound.

Her hand went to her mouth, searching for the hole.

It was tiny. The tiniest of tears, ripped into the plastic by her teeth.

But it was enough. She thrust her fingernails

into the tiny tear and pulled in opposite directions with all her might.

This time, the ripping sound was more substantial, and the black plastic parted, leaving a big enough hole for her to draw in huge, grateful gulps of fresh air.

The blue and orange spots evaporated.

Continuing to pull, she ripped the plastic away from her face and yanked the divided pieces down around her neck. The sun's brightness blinded her, and cold, fresh air surrounded her. She drank it in gratefully.

Weak and shaking, Jo sank to the ground. She knelt there, shaking, for long minutes.

When she had calmed down a little, she bent her chin to look down at the thick strips of black still wrapped around her neck. They hung there like a muffler, a grim reminder of how close she had come to death.

But . . . he hadn't meant to kill her, had he? If he had, he would have tied her arms so she would have no way of freeing herself. If he'd done that, she'd be dead now. As dead as Sharon Westover. . . .

Jo gasped. Whoa! Hold the phone. No one had said Sharon Westover was dead. They'd simply said that she had disappeared.

But she *was* dead. Jo *knew* it. Suddenly, clearly, emphatically, she knew that Sharon

Westover would never be seen alive on campus again.

As shaky as a newborn colt, Jo got to her feet. Ignoring the bag still wound around her neck, she walked as quickly as she could back to Lester. People running or walking across campus stared at her, and some laughed, but Jo ignored them. She was used to the staring by now, and she had more important things on her mind than how she looked to other people. It really didn't matter. Not now.

Jo's room was empty. She wasn't surprised. On a beautiful Saturday afternoon, why would anyone be inside? But she was disappointed. She didn't want to be alone just now.

A minute later, as if her wish had been heard and granted, Kelly and Nan burst into the room, laughing. The laughter stopped when they saw Jo standing in the middle of the room, struggling with the knot at the back of her neck.

"What is *that*?" Kelly cried. "It looks like . . ."

"A garbage bag," Nan finished, hurrying over to help Jo with the rope. "What is it doing around your *neck*?"

"Jo," Kelly said, as Nan worked on the knot, "your face is bleeding again." She couldn't hide the expression of distaste on her face. "It's a mess."

"I know. I scratched it when I was trying to get this thing off my head."

Kelly's eyes widened. "That bag was on your *head*? Over your face?"

Jo nodded. The knot came free and Nan unwound the rope and held it up triumphantly. "It pays to have long nails," she said. "Now tell us what's going on. How did this thing," unwrapping the black plastic from Jo's shoulders and removing it, "get on your head? That was a serious knot, Jo. Someone meant that rope to stay tied for a good long time."

Jo tottered over to her bed and flung herself down on it. "I know." Her voice was low and hushed. "I really thought I was going to die."

"Jo!"

She lifted her head and stared at both of them with tear-brightened eyes. "I mean it. I couldn't breathe. Someone ran up behind me on the path behind Butler Hall, threw that bag over my head, and tied that rope around it so tightly, the plastic was smashed into my mouth and nose. I *couldn't* breathe! He said . . . he said I shouldn't go out without a bag over my head, and then he ran away. I tried . . . I tried to get the knot untied, but I don't have long nails like you, Nan, and I couldn't do it."

"How did you get it off your face?" Kelly asked. She moved toward the bathroom. "I'll get you some clean bandages for your cuts."

"I bit through the plastic." Jo made a face. "It tasted horrible. But it was the only thing I could think of." She forced a weak laugh. "And I'm never going anywhere again without a very sharp nail file in my pocket."

Kelly came out of the bathroom with a handful of white gauze. "You'd better go wash off those cuts and put fresh tape on them. They look awful."

As Jo got up to obey, she couldn't help wondering if Kelly was being kind, or if she really couldn't stand the sight of Jo's face. And this time, Jo didn't feel guilty about wondering. *Someone* on campus viciously hated the sight of her. It could be anyone. Anyone at all. Even Kelly Benedict.

All Jo knew for sure was, it had to be someone who had a problem with flawed faces like hers. Which probably meant her attacker *had* no flaws. And that certainly applied to Kelly.

But Kelly was her friend and roommate. She'd never been anything but friendly and nice to Jo.

True. But she'd never hidden her distaste for what had happened to Jo's face, either. It really seemed to bother her.

The question was, how *much* did it bother Kelly?

"So," Jo asked casually when she came out of the bathroom with fresh bandages, "did you two go shopping?" Meaning, have you been together all afternoon so that I don't have to suspect my best friend and roommate of trying to suffocate me?

Nan shook her head. "We ran into each other out in the hall. I had a paper to finish. Jo," she said then, "what are you going to do about this? Don't you think you should call the police?"

Jo sat back down on the bed. "I don't know. I was going to. And I was going to tell them. . . ." Suddenly, telling anyone else, even her best friends, that she knew Sharon Westover was dead, seemed like a really bad idea. After all, she had no proof. No information. Only a conviction, stronger than any feeling she'd ever had. But. . . .

"What?" Kelly asked. "What else were you going to tell them?"

"Nothing." Jo shook her head. "I just don't think I can call the police and tell them that someone fastened a plastic bag over my head. How could they possibly take me seriously?"

"Maybe that was the whole idea," Nan said slowly. "Maybe whoever did it thought it was so outrageous, no one would believe you. So he'd get away with it. But you've got the plastic bag, Jo, and the rope. That's evidence. And it *was* a deliberate attack. The police should know about it."

Jo looked down at her hands, in her lap. "It would help if someone else had seen something. But there wasn't anyone around." She glanced at the telephone on her nightstand. "There *is* someone who might know something, though. I'm going to call Tina and see if she can tell me if someone pushed her. If she *was* pushed down those stairs, that's more ammunition to take to the cops, right?"

"She might not be able to talk on the phone yet," Kelly said. "But go ahead and try. That's a good idea."

Evan arrived as Jo was dialing. Kelly let him in. He noticed the torn bag and the rope right away. An inquisitive look on his face, Evan sat on the floor, frowning as Jo asked to speak to Tina Downs.

"Tina?" Jo gently fingered the bandages on her face. The cuts were hurting again. "This is Jo Donahue. How are you?"

"Drowsy. They gave me something. But I guess I'm okay, Jo. My head hurts, but that shouldn't surprise me, right? Slamming into a stone wall headfirst will do that." Tina paused, and then added, "I heard I slammed into you, too, Jo. Sorry. Are you okay?"

"Sure." Well, not really. But Tina didn't need to know that. She had enough problems of her own. "Tina, I was wondering . . ." Now that she had Tina on the phone, Jo wasn't sure what to ask. If Tina *hadn't* been pushed, if she'd simply slipped and fallen, she'd want to know why Jo was asking.

But Tina was the only one who could help her out now. She *had* to ask.

"Tina, what happened last night? Do you remember?"

"Yes, I remember, Jo. I wish I didn't. I wish I could forget, because it doesn't make any sense. No sense at all."

Jo's heart began pounding. "What happened? What happened that doesn't make any sense, Tina?"

Tina took a deep breath. "I was pushed down those stairs, Jo."

Jo sat up very straight.

"What?" Evan hissed. "What'd she say?"

Jo shook her head at him. "Are you sure, Tina?"

"Of course I'm sure. I'd heard Cath mention that there was more soda in the cellar, and I was going down to get some. But all of a sudden, someone shoved me, hard. I didn't have time to grab onto the railing. I didn't even have time to scream."

"Oh, Tina, I'm sorry," Jo breathed.

"Jo . . ." Tina hesitated. "Jo, that's not the worst of it."

Jo's heart sank into her stomach. "It's not?" She knew she didn't want to hear what the "worst of it" was. But she couldn't hang up now. She *had* to know. "What was, Tina? What was the worst of it?"

"Well, I didn't realize it until this afternoon, when I had time to think about it. But the person who pushed me whispered something as he came up behind me. I . . . I wasn't going to tell you, because I didn't want to scare you."

You *are* scaring me, Jo thought, gripping the receiver so tightly her wrist ached.

"But you have to know, so you can decide what to do." Tina paused again.

"Tina!" Jo cried from between clenched teeth. "*What* did he say?"

Another deep breath made its way through the phone line. Then, "He said, *'I told you not to go running around without your face covered up, Johanna.'*"

Jo let out a soft moan and sagged back against the wall.

"I'm sorry, Jo. I didn't want to tell you. But I thought you should know."

Jo said nothing, but the hand holding the receiver was shaking.

"It wasn't *me* he was after, Jo," Tina said. "It was *you*."

Chapter 16

When Jo hung up the telephone, her eyes bleak, Evan and Nan pressed her for information.

"What's wrong?" Evan asked, getting up to come and sit beside Jo on the bed. "You look like you just saw the proverbial ghost."

I did, Jo thought despairingly . . . my *own*.

"What did Tina say?" Nan pressed, standing in the middle of the room, hairbrush in hand. "Is she okay?"

She is, but *I'm* not, Jo said to herself. Aloud, she said, "I guess she's okay. Has a headache. But she . . ." Jo lifted her head, meeting Evan's eyes with her own ". . . she says she *was* pushed down those stairs."

"You're kidding!" Nan cried. "Is she sure?"

"Yes, and that's not the only thing she's sure of. She also said the person who pushed her called her Johanna."

"Johanna?" Kelly looked puzzled.

Jo nodded.

Evan's expression became grim. "He called her that," he said, "because he thought Tina *was* Jo. They were both wearing black, and with the kitchen light off. . . ." He took Jo's hand in his. "It *was* you he thought he was pushing, wasn't it?"

"According to Tina, it was. So it was probably the same creep who put that bag over my head. Tried to suffocate me."

They sat in nervous silence for a moment or two, then Jo looked straight at Evan and said, "Evan, someone is trying to kill me. Someone wants me dead."

"That's crazy!" Kelly cried. She plopped down on her own bed and faced Jo. "Why would anyone want you dead?"

"I don't know. That's what's driving me crazy. I *don't* know. But . . . but it's got something to do with my face." Jo glanced at the dresser mirror. "That's why the mirrors were covered. And then I got the hat with the veil and the corrective makeup . . . it's pretty obvious, don't you think? Someone *hates* what's happened to my face."

"Well, I hate it, too," Kelly said fervently, and then, her cheeks flushing, quickly added, "I mean, I hate that it happened to you. But I certainly wouldn't *kill* you rather than look at it . . . at you. That's just plain . . ."

"Crazy?" Jo interrupted. "Of course it's crazy. Pushing someone down a flight of stairs is crazy. I never said the person doing this stuff was sane. He's not. That's what scares me."

Evan pressed her then to call the police, but Jo said, "I don't have to. They're coming to see *me*. Tina told them what she heard just before she fell. So they're coming out here tomorrow to question me, see if I have any idea who might have done it." She shrugged. "I don't, so talking to them is going to be a waste of time."

"Are you going to tell them about what happened today?" Kelly asked.

"I guess so. I'll feel silly, but I'm sure it's all part of the same thing, so yeah, I guess I have to. I just hope they don't laugh."

"They won't," Evan assured her. He stood up, forced a smile. "Well, since we know the strong right arm of the law is going to be handling things from here on in, and since we can't do much about any of this until you talk to them, why don't we put all this on a back burner and go find some fun? It's a premium Saturday afternoon, and you'll be safe with all of us, Jo. How about it? Reed and Carl are skating down at the pond. Feel like joining them?"

Jo loved ice-skating. She'd been skating since she was eight. She'd been delighted when she found out that Salem University's duck pond, out behind the infirmary, was kept snow-free for skating whenever the ice was safe.

What better way to banish from her mind the awful plastic bag episode than to stride across the ice in her skates, feeling the sunshine on her face? Evan was right: she'd be safe on the pond, with so many people around her. She'd come home late, lock the door, go to bed, and when she got up Sunday morning, she'd hand the whole ugly business over to the police, who would know what to do.

"Yes," she said firmly, "I am definitely up for some ice-skating." Why should she stay in her room like some frightened rabbit? That would be giving the creep too much power. "Kelly? Nan? Are you coming?"

They nodded and went to change into suitable skating clothes.

"We'll change and meet you at the pond in fifteen minutes," Jo told Evan.

"Thirty," Kelly said firmly. "I can't get ready in less than thirty minutes, Jo, you know that."

"She's right," Jo said, smiling. "Meet you in thirty-five."

By the time they got outside, the sun had

disappeared and ominous gray clouds were sailing rapidly toward campus.

"It's going to snow," Kelly said. "I can smell it in the air. Oh well, it'll be fun skating while white stuff is coming down. We'll feel like we're on a Christmas card, right?"

"Unless it comes down too thick and fast," Nan pointed out as they trudged toward the pond. "If it does, we'll have to find something else to do."

If it does, Jo thought, my tape's going to get all wet and then I'll have to come back to the dorm for new bandages. Should have brought some with me, just in case.

The pond was crowded. The long, wide oval of ice sat at the foot of a steep slope behind campus, in a clearing surrounded by a wooded grove. Thick with skaters, the scene did remind Jo of a Christmas card, except that the pond was circled now not by pure white snow, but with dead grass and a few patches of old snow here and there.

Judging from the look of the darkening sky, that would change very quickly. "If we're going to get any skating in," she told Nan and Kelly, "we'd better get our skates on in a hurry. It's going to start snowing any second now."

The words were barely out of her mouth before a few random flakes began drifting down, and minutes later, the skies opened up and snow began falling thick and fast.

But Kelly had been right: it *was* fun skating through the cloud of white, like speeding across the ice through a wall of white cotton candy. Several people ran to get brooms from their dorms, and skated around the ice pushing the brooms in front of them in a light-hearted effort to keep the ice clear.

The ice-clearing efforts quickly became a fast and furious game of hockey, with the brooms as sticks and someone's wallet the puck.

Jo and Evan skated together, holding hands and circling the pond several times to music blaring from a cassette recorder someone had brought.

"Isn't this better than sitting in your room alone?" Evan cried over the music as they rounded a corner. "Fresh air and exercise can cure almost anything, right?"

Jo grinned and nodded. It *was* a great feeling, sailing along to the music, holding Evan's hand. She'd almost forgotten. . . .

She didn't even notice how wet the tape and bandages had become until Evan left to get her a cup of hot chocolate from the Sigma Tau concession stand. Now that she was standing still, she could feel the cold stinging her cheeks. She slipped her glove off and tentatively explored. One cut was exposed. She could feel its rough edges. The tape must have slipped off while she was skating.

A second later, another piece slid sideways under the touch of her fingers, and fell to the ground.

Darn.

It probably wasn't a good idea to leave the cuts uncovered, even though the snow and wind had lessened somewhat. She didn't want to make things worse when she was so close to having the stitches removed.

When Evan returned with her hot drink, Jo had a painful moment. The look in his eyes when he saw her uncovered injuries was one of shock. He covered up quickly, handing her the drink with some comment about how long the line had been at the concession stand, but it didn't help.

Telling herself she shouldn't be so sensitive, she took the drink, thanking him. After all, it probably *did* look pretty disgusting. Evan was human. Why shouldn't he have a reaction?

"I'm going to have to go fetch some fresh tape," she told him. "The infirmary's closer than Lester, so I'm going to run over there. I'll be right back."

She expected him to argue with her. Hadn't he said she'd "be safe" with them? Shouldn't he try to stop her from climbing the hill alone?

But just then the "puck" hit Evan in the left leg. Someone thrust a broom into his hands and, calling out to Jo that he'd wait for her there, he took off across the ice.

Jo watched him skate away, not sure whether to be amused or angry. The garbage bag episode had happened only a few hours earlier, but even to her, it seemed a long time ago. The sun had been shining then, it hadn't been snowing . . . it was almost as if the incident had taken place on an entirely different day. They'd had so much fun skating, they'd all forgotten that it had even happened.

Well, *she* hadn't. She'd been watching . . . paying attention . . . staying close to Evan or with Nan or Reed or Kelly or Carl. *She* hadn't forgotten. How could she?

But Evan had . . . or he wouldn't have let her go off to the infirmary by herself.

She should ask Nan or Kelly to come along. Safety in numbers . . .

But the infirmary was right at the top of the hill, right on the other side of that new wall. She'd be in plain sight of the pond almost the whole time. The snow wasn't coming down so hard now . . . they'd be able to see her.

And hadn't she decided she wasn't going to let that creep dictate how she lived her life?

She would go by herself. If whoever it was was watching, let him. He couldn't do anything to her in full view of all those people on the pond. And he'd see that he hadn't scared her into hiding. Maybe that would dent his ego so badly, he'd give up on her.

Trying to ignore a trace of resentment toward Evan for forgetting that she was in danger, Jo removed her skates, slung them over her shoulder, and hiked up the hill to the infirmary.

Dr. Trent wasn't on duty, and the nurse who greeted Jo at the front desk, added quickly, "I've got an emergency. One of your professors had an urge to be eighteen again. Went skating, fell on the ice, and sprained an ankle. Bandages and tape are in the back room, in the closet. Just jot down in the book whatever you take, okay? Makes it easier to keep track of inventory."

Glad to be in out of the cold, Jo headed straight for the back room where the supplies were kept. She would fix her bandages and take some extra in case the snow got heavier again. Then she could keep skating until it got dark. Later, maybe they'd all go to Vinnie's.

For a day that had started in such a horrible way, it had certainly improved.

She found the supply cabinet. Opened the

door. Reached inside for the packet of fresh white bandages, wrapped in plastic for sterility . . .

She was about to turn around when, for the second time that day, an arm came out of nowhere and wrapped itself around her neck, cutting off her air supply.

Chapter 17

Before Jo could make a sound, she was thrown into a wooden chair and her hands were quickly and roughly tied behind her back. Too shocked to think clearly, she cast a desperate glance over her shoulder. She caught only a glimpse of a figure all in black, face hidden behind a black ski mask. The glimpse told her nothing . . . except that she was in real danger.

"You just wouldn't listen, would you?" a voice whispered in her ear. *"I warned you and I warned you and I warned you."* There was a sharp tug on the ropes around her wrists to make sure they were tight enough. *"You just ignored me. I don't like that, Jo. I don't like that at all. I made a mistake, being so patient with you. I don't often make mistakes. And I hate it when I do."*

"What do you want?" Jo managed. Her legs weren't tied, but that did her no good at all.

Kicking backward would be futile. All she'd hit would be the chair legs. She would have to wait and hope he'd move out in front of her, where a well-placed foot might connect, might even do some damage.

The ski-masked head leaned in close to hers. She could feel the thick wool rubbing against her ear. *"What do I want? I want you to stop offending people with the sight of that ghastly face of yours. You won't do it on your own, like I wanted you to, so I'll have to do it for you."* And then, *"Don't even think about screaming. If you make a sound, I'll snap your neck like a twig."*

Jo's heart rolled over. She fell silent, biting on her lower lip to hold back the scream rising up in her throat.

She felt the figure behind her move away from her chair. A faint flicker of hope that he had finished with her, that he had only meant to scare her, died quickly as soft footsteps returned a minute later to take up a position behind her again.

What was he *doing* back there?

Maybe the nurse would need supplies, would come rushing into the room, see him, *stop* him. Or run and call the police before he could block her path.

That seemed Jo's only hope.

Something soft touched the top of her head. Something white rolled down over her shoulder, into her lap. She looked down. Narrow gauze bandage, unrolling itself across her shoulder, her lap, onto her thighs, a soft white ribbon tracing a path down her body.

Now it's not sterile anymore, she thought with an odd feeling of detachment born of shock. The wrapper is off and the gauze is touching my clothes and the floor and it's probably already covered with germs.

Then she almost laughed aloud. Like it mattered . . . he was probably going to kill her, anyway, right here in the infirmary supply room. Hadn't he said he had to "stop" her from showing her face in public? Hadn't it sounded like he meant . . . *permanently*? As in *forever*?

"Stop shaking," he ordered in that same ominous whisper. *"I can't do this right if you won't sit still."*

Couldn't do *what* right? What was he doing with that gauze?

Then she felt it. Hands on the top of her head, the softness of gauze being wound around her head, across her forehead, then around her head again, and again across her forehead. . . .

"I didn't want to have to do this, Jo. But you refused to understand how important it is for

the world to be a beautiful place. All you had
to do was stay inside until your bandages came
off. Was that so much to ask? I don't think so.
I did it for years, day in, day out, for years!
Never going outside in daylight where people
could see me and hate me for the way I looked.
I never even knew what the world really looked
like until I was twelve because for all those
years, I only saw it after dark. You can't see
much in the dark, Jo. Not much at all."

Jo gasped and instinctively kicked out with
her feet when the first layer of gauze reached
her eyes. Having her eyes covered was terrifying. "No," she cried, "no, don't!"

In answer, he jerked cruelly on the bandage.
"Shut up! I told you not to make a sound! If
that stupid nurse comes running in here, I'll
have to kill her. And you'll be responsible. So
shut your mouth."

"You didn't lock the door?" Jo asked, hope
in her voice.

"You need a key to lock it. Anyway, it
doesn't matter. The nurse is the only one here,
and she's busy. By the time she finishes with
that idiot, Professor Lang, I'll be long gone.
And it'll be too late for her to do anything for
you."

Another layer of gauze was wrapped around
her eyes, then another. She could no longer

see. Becoming suddenly blind was utterly terrifying.

"Forget about the door," came the voice in
her ear. *"You'd never make it. I'm faster than
you are, and my eyes aren't covered."*

If she'd known about the door sooner. . . .

"Quit kidding yourself," as if she'd said the
thought out loud. *"I'd never have let you get to
the door. That would have ruined everything."*

The wrapping continued, the gauze slowly,
efficiently winding around her cheekbones, her
nose. If it covered her nostrils, she would have
to breathe through her mouth. And if someone
didn't come, didn't help her, before it reached
her mouth . . . how would she breathe then?

She wouldn't.

Jo felt like she'd been kicked in the chest.
This . . . this was what he was doing? Wrapping
her like a mummy, suffocating her like he'd
tried to do with the plastic bag? But . . . but
that had only been a warning. He'd left her
hands untied so she could free herself.

Her hands were tied now.

This was no warning.

"Please," she whispered as the gauze, once,
twice, three times, circled her nose and effec-
tively shut off her ability to breathe through
her nostrils, "please. . . ."

"Please? Please?" A low, wicked chuckle.

"As in pretty please? For years, I thought when She said 'pretty please' to get me to do something, that She meant pretty things were pleasing to her. And I thought that was really cruel, considering what I looked like then. I was anything but pretty. It made no sense, her saying 'pretty please' to me, because She wasn't a cruel person, not at all. She was kind and protective. But I never, ever talked to any other human beings except Them, so how could I know that 'pretty please' just meant an extra please?"

The gauze covered the space between her nose and her upper lip. Once, twice, three times.

There was nothing she could do. Her hands were tied behind her back, and no matter how hard she tried to free them, the ropes failed to give. Her legs were free, but useless, with him standing behind her chair instead of in front of it. And screaming for help would just make him kill her more quickly.

"You don't know what it was like. Being trapped inside all those years. Never feeling the sun on your face, never playing with other children. But even when I was very small, I understood that They were doing the right thing. The world shouldn't have to see such ugliness.

"And They did it for my sake, too. Other chil-

dren would have made fun of me for the way I looked, tortured me, wounded me to the core. I would have been emotionally scarred forever by their cruelty. Knowing that, They protected me from it. They kept me safe. That's all I was trying to do for you, Jo. But you wouldn't let me. You ignored me. I thought you were smarter than that."

Any second now, the gauze would reach her mouth, cover her lips, shut off her air passages completely. She had to *do* something, had to *stop* it . . .

Before she could think of something, the fingers stopped, left her face. Footsteps padded away.

He'd run out of gauze. He'd gone to the cabinet for another roll.

She had maybe one split second in which to do *something*, anything . . .

If only she could see . . .

But she could use her legs. The chair she was tied to was lightweight wood, and only her wrists were fastened to it. She could lift it. If she moved quickly. . . .

Taking a deep breath through her mouth, Jo pulled herself to her feet, taking the chair with her. A few steps to the door. . . .

But she had never walked with a chair tied to her back. She lost her balance before she took even one step. Toppling sideways with a startled cry, she crashed to the floor, where she lay on her side, the chair still attached to her back by her wrists.

"What do you think you're doing?" The whisper was furious. *"You never learn, do you? You refuse to take me seriously! Sharon Westover could tell you that's a mistake, Johanna. Sharon could tell you that when I make up my mind to do something, it gets done."* Another evil chuckle. *"That is, if Sharon could still talk. Unfortunately, it's too late for Sharon to tell you anything. Too bad. Sorry about that."*

So she'd been right about Sharon. How horrible.

The chair, with Jo still fastened to it, was hoisted upright and slammed back into place.

Jo was dizzy. Her head reeled. And her stomach lurched as she realized she'd missed her only chance to escape.

"If you think your face looks bad, you should have seen hers. It was grotesque. She must have gone through the windshield. I couldn't believe it when she showed up on campus. Wasn't even bandaged. I sent her a hat with a veil, too, and a tube of that corrective makeup. She just ignored them. People said she had guts, coming back to school. But it wasn't guts. It was thoughtlessness. Cruelty . . . making people

*look at her. When she ignored my efforts to
protect her, to keep her away from offended
eyes, I knew I had no choice. It was her own
fault, Jo. Just like this is your own fault. You
should have listened to my warnings."*

Jo breathed heavily through her mouth. She
couldn't *see* the gauze on its way to cover her
mouth, but she could feel it. If she took a huge,
deep gulp of air and saved it, as if she were
about to dive underwater, maybe that would
buy her some time. Somehow she had to escape.

But Sharon Westover hadn't. She was dead.
And the figure in black who was now beginning
to wind the gauze around Jo's mouth was responsible.

She was trapped in this small white room
with a cold-blooded killer.

Who meant to kill her, too.

Here came the gauze over her lips. He
yanked it in tightly, to cut off any possibility
of her breathing through her mouth.

With only one layer of porous gauze over her
mouth, she was still able to breathe, though
erratically. But as the second layer pressed itself harshly against her lips, she knew she had
only minutes to live.

Now that she could no longer see, he had
moved from behind her over to her right side.

She could feel him moving near her right arm.

If she was going to do something, it had to be *now*.

She leaned back in her chair, lifted both legs high, and quickly brought them back down, slamming them onto the floor as hard as she could while at the same time, throwing herself backward. The push of her feet against the floor combined with the weight of her body leaning to the rear, sent the chair toppling a second time, but this time backward.

She landed on her back.

And although she couldn't see, she knew he was bending over her. The curses he uttered told her where his head was. She brought both legs up and kicked out with a fury born of desperation.

And connected. A startled, angry "Ooof!" told her the breath had been knocked out of her target. She had missed the head but probably hit the chest. Footsteps staggered backward, there was a crashing sound, and then something hit the hard wooden floor.

Jo scrambled up, yanking the chair up with her, and raced for where she thought the door should be. She ran right into it, the doorknob jabbing her cruelly in the stomach when she and the door collided.

But she couldn't open it. Tears of frustration

melded into the gauze over her eyes as she faced her helplessness. Even if she turned around, her back to the door, the chair tied to her wrists would prevent her from reaching the doorknob.

Scrambling sounds behind her told her time was running out.

She did whirl around then so that her back was to the door, and began crazily, wildly, slamming the chair legs against the wooden door.

And it opened.

"Okay if I fill my thermos with water in here?" a deep, male voice asked, and then, in a totally different voice, said, "What . . . what the hell?"

There was a scuttling sound off to Jo's left, then the sound of another door opening, slamming shut, and then silence.

He was gone.

Chapter 18

Dissolving in relief, Jo fell to her knees on the floor.

"Hey, what is this?" the deep voice behind her cried. "Some dumb college stunt or something? You look like a mummy."

"Please," Jo begged, "please . . . get this off."

She didn't know who it was that knelt beside her, unwrapping the gauze, removing the chair, but she didn't care. All she knew for sure was that it wasn't *him*. He'd gone, left by a back door she hadn't even known was there.

Gone . . . for now. . . .

But he wasn't finished with her. That was another thing she knew for sure.

When her eyes were free, she saw, kneeling beside her, a huge man in a plaid jacket, a red hardhat on his head.

No wonder her attacker had run away. What

she saw before her was no small, thin nurse, easily disposed of. The man in the hardhat was the size of a truck.

"You playing some kind of game here?" the man repeated as he helped Jo to her feet. He frowned in disapproval. "Looks kind of sick to me."

"No," she said, sinking gratefully down into the chair he'd uprighted for her. "It wasn't a game. That . . . that person who ran away when you opened the door tried to kill me. Could you please call the police?"

The police barraged her with questions. Most of them she couldn't answer. No, she didn't recognize him. He was wearing a ski mask. No, she didn't recognize his voice. He had whispered.

But she did tell them what he had said about Sharon Westover.

"Well," one police officer told another, "that's no surprise. The girl hasn't turned up anywhere. We knew the chances were good that we were talking homicide here, right?"

It was only later, when they'd finally escorted her back to her room and left, that Jo remembered one thing that had been whispered to her. "I thought you were smarter than that, Jo," the voice had said.

The room was empty. Kelly and Nan and the

others must have gone to eat without her.

"I thought you were smarter than that, Jo. . . ."

So it *was* someone she knew. At least . . . someone who knew *her*.

How well did you need to know someone to know how smart they were?

Maybe all it meant was that he was in one of her classes . . . a class she did well in . . . English, maybe, or chem.

Maybe all it meant was, he'd heard someone *say*, "Jo Donahue is no dummy." It could be something as simple as that, couldn't it?

Or . . . Jo sat up . . . it could mean that he was someone she knew *well*.

How well?

Well enough to know what room she lived in. Well enough to know she would be at Cath's party, and what she would be wearing at that party. Okay, so he'd made a mistake and pushed Tina instead of her, but that *was* a mistake. He'd thought it was her.

As for the rest of it, he must have been following her. That's how he knew she'd gone down to the riverbank, and over to the infirmary. He'd been watching to see if she heeded his warnings and hid in her room, the way he wanted her to.

Jo shuddered and wrapped her arms around

her chest. Yes, that had to be it. Because she
hadn't *planned* to walk along the riverbank.
That hike had been an afterthought, and she'd
told no one ahead of time. So he couldn't have
known that. He'd simply been following her,
and gone where she'd gone.

And he was still out there . . . waiting . . .
for her. . . .

Jo glanced around the room, and noticed the
note on the mirror.

She got up and walked over to read it.

> *Starving. At Burgers Etc. We waited
>   forever for you.*
> *One of us will come back to pick you
>   up so you can eat, too. Hope you got
>   your bandages okay.*
>
> *Kelly*

The mere thought of food made Jo ill. And
she didn't think she'd ever leave the safety of
her room again.

Chapter 19

Of all the luck! That stupid Neanderthal had to show up just when I was getting to the finish line with Jo. Another minute or two and she'd have been history.

Johanna will tell the police what I said about Sharon. No problem. Jo doesn't know who I am, and neither do they. And what fun is it disposing of blights on the landscape if no one knows about it? I'm glad I told her.

Jo's a fighter, I'll give her that. Westover was so much easier. Anyway, I was doing her a favor. She could never, ever have been happy in this world. Not with that face.

They'll never find her. I made sure of that.

So let Johanna tell the police anything she wants.

I'm not worried.

Worry makes frown lines.

Now, about Jo. . . .

Chapter 20

Jo walked over to the window. Darkness had fallen, and the old-fashioned pole lights on campus cast lemon-colored rays across a thin blanket of fresh new snow. The storm had ended as quickly as it began, and the navy blue sky had cleared, revealing a sliver of moon and an abundance of stars.

Such a peaceful-looking night. So deceptive. . . .

As she turned away from the window, she caught a glimpse of her reflection in the dresser mirror. She had forgotten to replace the tape that had fallen off at the pond. Two of the deeper cuts on her cheeks were laid bare.

She walked over to the mirror and calmly studied what she saw there. Not a pretty sight. The bandage under her eye, dampened by snowflakes, drooped, soggy as wet toast. Two pieces of clear tape were peeling away from her skin, and the uncovered cuts still had a rawness to them, like fresh meat.

Her face was the reason he was after her. Just as the damage done to Sharon Westover's face in that car wreck was the reason she was no longer alive.

It made no sense. But it was true.

Jo turned away from the mirror. What good did it do her to know the reason for the attacks on her? How did that help?

She could point it out to the police. Maybe it would somehow help them find the person responsible.

A sharp rapping on the door startled her, set her heart pounding. Then she remembered Kelly's note. Someone was supposed to come and collect Jo, take her to Burgers to join her friends.

She didn't want to go. Not now. She wouldn't be safe there, not even in a crowd.

"Jo? You in there?"

Evan's voice.

On the other hand, she didn't want to spend any more time alone, either.

She hurried to the door and let him in.

"Where have you been?" he asked. His cheeks were still red from ice-skating. "We've been looking all over for you. I went to the infirmary right after you left the pond, but the nurse said you'd come and gone."

"She probably thought I had. But I . . . I was still there. She just didn't know it."

"Still there?" Evan frowned. "We all left the pond right after you. We . . ." Evan's cheeks flushed, "we forgot about . . . well, I guess we forgot that we didn't want you to be alone. I'm sorry, Jo. You okay?"

"You all left the pond right after I did?" They hadn't been at the pond, still skating while she was being mummy-wrapped?

Her attacker had been someone who *knew* her. . . .

Evan nodded and sat down in Jo's desk chair. "Yeah. When you weren't at the infirmary, I went back to the pond. Nan and Kelly said they needed dry gloves, anyway, so they'd check to see if you were here. Reed said he'd stay at the pond, in case you went back there, and Carl went ahead to Burgers to see if you'd decided to get there ahead of us."

"I didn't even know we'd decided to go there," Jo protested.

"We thought maybe someone had mentioned it. Anyway, we all separated to hunt for you. Then we collected at Burgers. Obviously none of us had found you."

Uneasiness flooded Jo. She had thought all of her friends had been at the pond. She had thought they were together. But they weren't. They had separated.

Someone who knew her had tried to kill her. It couldn't be one of them. It couldn't.

"There wasn't any sign of you when we got to Burgers," Evan continued, frowning. "I was pretty steamed at myself for letting you take off for the infirmary alone, after everything that's happened. Couldn't believe I'd been that dense. We were all worried about you."

"Not as worried as *I* was," Jo said heavily. "You'd better sit down. This may take a few minutes."

When she had filled him in on her terrifying encounter in the infirmary storeroom, she fell silent. She found herself watching him for the tiniest hint that he wasn't surprised. But he looked stunned, and thoroughly shaken.

His windburned cheeks flushed a deeper red with anger. "He wrapped you up like a mummy? That's the sickest thing I've ever heard!"

"It's because of my face." Jo absentmindedly fingered a loose piece of tape. "The draped mirrors, the veiled hat, the tube of cover-up . . . all of those things were warnings that I shouldn't appear in public with my bare face hanging out. When I ignored the warnings, he decided to punish me."

"Oh, come on, Jo," Evan said in disbelief, "your face isn't that bad. A few cuts, a bruise or two . . . that's not enough to make someone try to *kill* you!"

Jo shrugged. "I think it is. There's more, Evan. He *did* kill Sharon Westover. The girl who was in that bad car crash last fall? Dr. Trent told me she'd been disfigured. And while he was turning me into a mummy, he admitted that he'd warned Sharon, too, and that she'd ignored him just like I did. So he said he shut her up permanently. His exact words were 'Unfortunately, it's too late for Sharon to tell you anything.' That's pretty clear, isn't it?"

"Did you tell the police that?"

"Of course."

Evan thought for a minute. "Did you get a look at this weirdo?"

"No. Not really. He was dressed all in black, just like Tina at Cath's party. He even had a black ski mask on, just like she did. Maybe that's where he got the idea. Anyway, I couldn't begin to tell the police what he looked like. I don't even remember how tall he was, I was so scared."

Evan made a sound low in his throat, and put an arm around her. "Look, forget about eating. If we get hungry, we'll go down to the cafe and get something. But I'm not leaving you here alone. I'll stay, at least until Kelly gets back, okay?"

Jo nodded. Definitely okay.

"I never should have let you go to the infirmary alone," he said then, his mouth set in a grim, straight line. "I wasn't thinking. . . ."

"It's okay. I thought I was perfectly safe. Not your fault."

"If anything had happened to you. . . ." Flushing guiltily, Evan put his head in his hands, his eyes on the floor.

"Evan." Jo reached over and gently dislodged his hands, turning his face toward her. "I'm okay. I'm fine, really." Then, because he didn't look convinced, she bent forward impulsively and kissed him. A strong, healthy, I'm-not-a-victim kiss.

"Now do you believe me?" she asked.

He relaxed then. She could see some of the tension ease out of his face. "I'm not sure," he said in a slow, thoughtful voice. "I don't think I'm quite convinced yet."

Jo laughed.

When Evan was finally convinced that she really was okay, they talked about the puzzle at length. They agreed that Jo's tormentor was someone she knew. But she could know him only casually. They wondered if he was watching her all the time, or only occasionally.

And, most important, just how crazy *was* he? Because they both agreed that someone who would harm two people who had already been victims had to be totally, completely insane.

"You don't remember anything about him?" Evan persisted. "Think, Jo! It's important. Right now, we don't have any way of knowing who it is. So how can you feel safe anywhere, any time? If you don't think of something, you're going to have to stay locked in your room until the cops come up with something. Can't you give them anything to go on?"

She was still thinking when Nan and Kelly, Carl and Reed showed up at the door. Kelly was carrying two white paper sacks and Carl was balancing two drinks. The heavenly aroma coming from the paper sacks revived Jo's appetite. She accepted gratefully, feeling a twinge of guilt because as grateful as she was, she really hoped they wouldn't stay. She didn't want to have to tell her story again and, more than that, she wanted to be alone with Evan.

Kelly picked up on that right away and announced that Saturday night or not, she had some heavy-duty studying to do at the library. The other three took the hint, each giving a different, and barely believable, reason why they had to leave.

But before they left, Evan insisted on paying

them for the hamburgers and drinks. No one argued. Burgers Etc. was a great place to hang out, but the food wasn't cheap.

When Evan pulled a bill from his wallet, a slip of bright pink paper fell out and sailed to the floor.

Jo recognized it for what it was. She'd had dozens of those bright pink slips herself.

They were receipts from the beauty supply shop in town.

What was Evan doing with a receipt from a beauty supply shop?

Jo sucked in her breath. Now don't start thinking terrible things, she warned herself, don't go crazy here. There's an explanation . . .

When the others had gone, Evan stooped to retrieve the slip on the floor and stuffed it back into his wallet.

"Been buying beauty supplies, have you?" Jo asked lightly as she busied her shaking fingers with the white paper bag.

"Suntan lotion," he answered. "I figured I didn't want to repeat Tina's mistake. But I'm allergic to the stuff. Have to take it back, so I'm glad I kept the slip. Efficient of me, don't you think? Normally, I toss stuff like that the minute I get home."

Normally, normally, normally, Jo singsonged in her head . . . what was normal and what wasn't? Why had he done something this time that he didn't normally do? Why had he kept the slip?

If only she'd seen the date on it. If the date was *before* Tina got that sunburn. . . .

No. It wouldn't be. Evan was telling the truth. He *was*.

"Anything wrong?" he asked as they bit into their hamburgers. "I mean, I know there's plenty wrong, but . . . you're not disappointed that the rest of the crew took off, are you? I'm getting the feeling you'd rather not be alone with me. And I'm wondering where that feeling is coming from."

Jo couldn't answer him. Telling him that her face was itching like poison ivy, she excused herself and went into the bathroom to apply fresh gauze and tape.

As she pulled the box of gauze pads from the medicine cabinet, she thought sadly that she couldn't fool Evan. He *knew* something was very wrong.

She should simply ask him if she could see the pink receipt. He'd understand, wouldn't he? After all, she'd almost lost her *life*. This was no time to ignore something as important as that slip of pink paper could be.

She had to do something, because her suspicion about Evan was making her sick.

Jo faced the mirror to begin working on her face.

Where was Sharon? Where had she been hidden? The maniac in the ski mask had said she was where no one would ever find her. Had he hidden her somewhere on campus, or had he taken her far away where no one would think to look for her?

Insane . . . he was insane.

Jo shivered, suddenly chilled to the bone. He was insane . . . and it was *her* he was after now.

Still, there *was* a difference. Sharon had been alone. She apparently hadn't told anyone what was going on in her life. Because if she *had*, they would have told the police about it when Sharon first disappeared.

The police *hadn't* heard about it, Jo was sure of that. She could tell by the way they had exchanged surprised looks when she'd filled them in on her own warning "messages."

Sharon had had to go through all of that by herself. But, Jo thought, bending her head over the sink to measure and cut a properly sized piece of tape, I'm not alone. The police know what's happening, and so do my friends.

The problem is . . . I'm suddenly having trouble knowing who to trust. *That's* what this nut has done to me, and I hate him for that almost as much as I do for everything else he's done.

Suddenly not trusting good friends was almost as bad as being physically threatened.

Sighing heavily, Jo cut the piece of tape and lifted her head to the medicine cabinet mirror to help her position the tape correctly.

But as her eyes met the glass, her mouth dropped open and a sound that was half gasp, half muffled scream filled the small, silent, white-tiled room.

Her face was not the only reflection in the mirror. There was another.

Someone was standing directly behind her left shoulder.

Someone wearing a black ski mask.

Chapter 21

"Hi, there, Johanna," a voice whispered in Jo's ear as she stared into the mirror, with disbelieving eyes. "Fancy meeting you here. What's new?"

She whirled then, prepared to run, but a strong arm grabbed her and spun her back against the sink. "You're not going anywhere," the voice hissed. "Not until I say so. And don't even think about screaming. It will be the last sound you ever make."

The eyes in the ski mask were blue. Deep, bright blue.

Like Evan's. . . .

No! Not Evan. It couldn't be Evan.

But . . . no one else had been in her room. Only Evan.

Desperate to erase the terrible thought, Jo strained to remember if she had heard anything after she left the room. Even the slightest sound could have been someone else joining Evan.

But she knew she had heard nothing.

He spun her around again, so that she was facing the mirror. One hand came from behind her to shove her head down, forcing her to stare into the sink, while another hand shoved a scratchy black object into her hands.

The ski mask.

"Put this on," came the whispered demand. "Backwards. I'll be leading the way, so you don't need to see." And then, cruelly, "And I certainly don't want to see *your* face. Cover it *up!*"

He had taken off the mask. It was in her hands. If she whipped her head around before he could stop her, she would finally know the identity of her attacker.

Guessing what she had in mind, both hands reached out from behind her, grabbed the mask, and before she could move, thrust the scratchy wool down over her head, over her face. Backwards.

She could see nothing.

"We're going to take a little walk. And I hate to sound like a bad television show, but if you try anything, Johanna, it'll be the last thing you ever do." A crazy cackle and then, "Of course, if you're in a *hurry* to die, I'd be glad to oblige. It's your choice."

"No," she said, moving away from the sink, "no. . . ."

"Then *go!*" He pushed her roughly, through the doorway and out into the room.

Only minutes earlier, she had been sitting there, talking and laughing with Evan as they ate their hamburgers.

She hadn't heard anyone else come in. . . .

He didn't like old houses because they weren't new and perfect. Did he feel the same way about damaged faces? He said he hadn't found her at the infirmary.

Was he lying?

He had said the pink receipt from the beauty supply shop was for sunscreen. Because of Tina's blistered lips. He didn't want the same thing to happen to him, he'd said. But the day she'd thought he was going into the sporting-goods store, the day that he'd probably gone into the beauty supply shop instead, was the day they'd rented the costumes. That was *before* they'd gone skiing. He wouldn't have been worried about sunburn then. If only she'd caught a glimpse of the date on that receipt. Then she'd know for sure.

Reed had pointed out, early on, that she didn't know Evan all that well. She'd been irritated with Reed. She should have paid closer attention to what he was saying.

But whether or not her captor was Evan, he had *killed* Sharon Westover, and had promised to do the same to her. Now, he was here to carry out his promise.

A tiny ray of hope warmed her as he shoved her across the room, in the direction of the door. He wasn't going to kill her here and now. He was going to take her *out* of the room. They could meet someone in the hallway, or on the stairs or in the elevator. The minute she heard another person's voice, she would *run*. He wasn't wearing a mask now. If it really *was* Evan, he was well known on campus. Without a mask, he'd be recognized. So he wouldn't dare do anything to her in front of someone.

She'd be safe.

If they ran into anyone.

They didn't.

Her heart sank when she realized that he was taking her down the fire stairs. Most people on the fourth floor used the elevator. They weren't likely to run into anyone on the stairs. He knew that, of course, just as she did.

But she refused to give up hope. Someone *could* be on the stairs. They would never let a person wearing a backwards ski mask pass by without a comment. The very second she heard a voice, she'd take off like a rocket. She'd rip the mask off her head, race to a telephone, and call the police.

Only one person, just one . . . that was all she needed.

But ño one was using the fire stairs that Saturday night.

No one.

She hadn't been counting the floors as they descended, but when she heard the creak of a door opening and cold wind against her face, she knew they were leaving the building. They had to be in the basement. No more stairs . . . no more hope of running into someone to save her.

A small sob caught in Jo's throat.

Frigid air slapped her in the face as the door to the outside swung open and she was pushed through it.

She gasped as cold stung her face, her arms, her ears. "I need a jacket," she complained, hardly aware of what she was saying.

The evil chuckle came again. "You've got to be kidding!" The door slammed shut behind them. He pushed her forward. Toward the parking lot, she thought. "You're worried about catching a cold?" Another laugh. "Well, of *course* you are. You wouldn't want to get pneumonia, Jo. Why, that could *kill* you!"

A flash of anger washed over Jo. She had *danced* with Evan, told him things she hadn't told anyone else, *kissed* him. She had . . . yes, she *had* thought she might be falling in *love* . . . crazy, crazy.

No! *She* wasn't the crazy one. *He* was.

If it was him. . . .

More than she'd ever wanted anything, she wanted it not to be Evan.

Another door opening . . . she was being pushed, into a . . . car? Yes, a car. Her elbow bumped against the steering wheel. She was being shoved in on the driver's side, and pushed across the seat to the passenger's side, leaving her no time in the car alone to escape.

And the last of her hope disappeared as she realized with a sinking heart that it was Evan's car. She smelled the lingering odors of his leather jacket, his spicy after-shave, his cinnamon gum. Unmistakable. When her right elbow bumped against the familiar nick in the arm rest on the passenger's door, she sagged against it, every trace of denial gone. She had scratched her elbow on that nick more than once.

Bitter tears stung Jo's eyelids.

Evan. . . .

Where was he taking her?

"Don't take that mask off," the chilling whisper warned as he climbed into the driver's seat. "Bad enough your face is a mess. You don't want a broken arm, too, do you? Leave the mask on."

"Evan, please," she said softly as the car started with a roar. "I don't know why you're doing this."

"Because you're ugly," came the answer. "I was hoping it was temporary, that that stupid doctor knew what she was talking about. But now, I don't think so." The car jerked out of the parking space and raced out of the lot. "It doesn't look to me like that's healing well at all. I've been patient long enough. Maybe too long."

"Why don't you stop whispering?" Jo said coldly. "I *know* who you are." It seemed useless to pretend she hadn't guessed his identity. He was going to kill her, anyway. And then he was going to put her wherever he'd put Sharon . . . where "no one would ever find her," he'd said. She, too, would be missing, and no one would know where she was.

And no one would suspect Evan. Never. No one would guess he was a killer. He'd make up some story about why he'd left her in her room alone . . . maybe he'd say they'd had an argument . . . and then he'd somehow establish an alibi. He was clever. Very, very clever.

She had liked that about him . . . his cleverness. But that was before she knew how twisted he was.

Suddenly, the car screeched to a stop. Jo sat up straight. They'd only been driving a minute or so. They had to still be on campus. He wasn't taking her somewhere far away?

"Turn and face the window," the whisper ordered.

Jo hesitated. Was he going to hit her on the back of the head? Choke her? Was he going to kill her *now*?

The thought that turning away from him might lead to her last moment alive, made it impossible for Jo to move. She sat frozen, her hands in her lap, too terrified to even tremble. She had been afraid all along . . . but she'd thought she had time. As long as they were walking, as long as they were driving, she had been able to resist the idea of . . . death.

She did not want to die. There were so many things she hadn't done yet . . . she wanted more time. Lots more time.

"I *said*, turn and face the window. I'm not going to kill you *here*, if that's what you're worried about. That would be stupid, and you should know by now, Johanna, I'm anything but stupid."

Relief turned her legs to water. She believed

him. She had more time. She wasn't going to die here, in Evan's car.

He didn't want to leave any clues in his own car.

She turned and faced the window.

"*Don't* turn around," she was warned. And in the next second, the black ski mask was ripped off her face and head.

She could *see*.

She didn't want to *see* Evan's face. Didn't want to come face-to-face with a harsh reality that she couldn't bear. Knowing the truth was one thing. Staring at it in the face was another.

You're still pretending, she scolded herself. You're still being stupid. *Look* at him! Make him see what's in your eyes. Give yourself that much satisfaction, before it's too late.

But when she swiveled her head around to look at him, it was too late. The ski mask was already on *his* head, covering everything but his eyes and mouth.

"I *want* you to be able to see now," he whispered, opening the car door on his side. "I want you to see everything that's happening to you. Come and see where I've brought you, Johanna. Come see your final resting place."

Chapter 22

Jo ignored the whispered command to leave the car. She was safer staying right where she was. He'd never be dumb enough to kill her in his own car. That would leave evidence. And he was already at risk. Nan and Kelly would tell the police they'd left her in her room with Evan. As the last person to see her alive, he'd be the *first* suspect. He couldn't afford to add to that suspicion by leaving evidence in his car.

She was staying put.

"Oh, no, you don't!" A hand reached into the car and latched onto her hair, fingernails cruelly digging into her scalp. "I said, get out, and I meant it! Now, haul your carcass out of there before I lose my temper."

She was dragged painfully across the front seat and yanked out of the car.

When she was standing upright, she glanced around. It was dark, but there were lights in the Quad, the huge dorm behind them, and there was a sliver of moonlight.

In the darkness ahead of them, giant, black objects loomed large and eerie in the pale light reflected from the dorm. Heavy construction equipment. Then she knew where they were. They were at the site of the new wall behind the infirmary. Their brief car trip had brought them to the construction site. The crew had gone home. The area that by day was busy, noisy, and messy, was now still and silent.

Why had he brought her here?

She didn't want to know.

Without a sweater or jacket, Jo was quickly frozen to the bone. She couldn't stop shaking, but she knew it wasn't only from the cold. Terror, too, was freezing the blood in her veins.

Keeping a tight grip on her right arm, her captor dragged her along the upturned dirt, through ragged ruts in the earth, to the newest section of the wall. Then, with a vicious shove against the back of her neck, Jo was forced to her knees beside a deep, open hole.

"They'll be pouring the cement tomorrow," the whisper told her. He handed her a long, thick stick with a sharp point. "Write your name!" he commanded. "In the bottom of the wall, there, where it's still wet. *Do* it!"

Feeling sick and sad that Evan, whom she

had thought was kind and sweet, could be so cruel, and terrified of the open hole gaping next to her, Jo began scrawling her name in the wet cement, holding the long, sharp stick in fingers that were numb with cold.

"That's your headstone," she was told. "Don't worry, you'll have company. Sharon's in that second section over there."

Trembling uncontrollably from both cold and fear, Jo glanced over her shoulder to see a black-gloved finger pointing toward a lower section of the stone wall. "Poor Sharon, she wasn't as lucky as you, Jo. No headstone. It wouldn't have been smart to put her name in the wall, with so much work yet to be done. Someone might have noticed. But," the whisper lightened, "tomorrow's the last day and the workmen will be so anxious to get out of here, they'll never notice your name. Besides, I'll cover it with dirt when we're . . . done here."

Thinking of Sharon buried in the cold, wet ground, Jo was overwhelmed with dizziness. Unable to remain upright, she sank back on her heels.

But a knee in her back urged her upright again. "Now, *write*! Quit stalling! I don't have all night!" An eerie giggle. "And trust me, neither do *you*!"

As Jo slowly scrawled her name in the damp

cement, the voice behind her whispered in a chillingly casual voice, "Sharon never knew what hit her. There she was, walking along campus with her head down, the way she always did so that no one could see her horrible face. She looked so totally miserable, I figured she was probably thinking how she'd like to go down to the old railroad bridge and jump off. So, if you think about it, I was doing the girl a favor, right?"

The stick moved slowly in the wet cement. J . . . O . . . H . . . A . . . "How did you kill her?" she asked in a hushed voice. She didn't really want to know, but keeping him talking might buy her some extra time.

"She never felt a thing." There was pride in the whisper. "I hit her from behind."

N . . . N . . . A . . . Why wasn't her name longer? Her middle name was Elizabeth. That would take a while. E . . . L . . .

"Hey, skip the middle name! I told you, I haven't got all night. You're taking too long as it is."

She etched out the E and the L, and began writing D . . . O . . . N . . . .

Satisfied, he whispered, "Listen, it was so funny. I brought her over here, and there was this great big hole, ready and waiting. I put her in there and filled in the hole halfway."

"You make me sick," Jo said forcefully. A . . . H. "What did that girl ever do to you?"

"I told you! She was ugly! You didn't see her, so don't start judging me. If you had, you'd see why I had to do it."

"No, I wouldn't. It wasn't her fault she looked that way. It was the accident."

"Well, *I* know that! I never said it was her fault. You just don't get it, do you, Jo? I wasn't *punishing* Sharon. I was *saving* her. From being an outcast. Just like I'm saving you. And saving the world from both of you. Why can't you understand that? Don't make me out to be a terrible person when I'm not!"

U . . . E. Done. She was done. She had written her name as slowly as she possibly could. Easy, when her fingers were numb with cold. But now . . .

"Put the date," came the whispered command. "A headstone should have a date."

Then, as she began printing numbers, the voice took on a dreamy, lilting quality. "It's going to be really pretty here. When the workmen have gone, I'm going to clean it up really nice, and when spring comes, I'm going to plant flowers. No one will ask why. Everyone knows I like things pretty. Pretty is the only thing that counts."

"Oh, it *is* not!" Jo shouted. "That's the

dumbest thing I've ever heard! Abraham Lincoln wasn't beautiful. Winston Churchill looked like a bulldog, and Eleanor Roosevelt would never have made Miss America. And those people *mattered*."

"Are you comparing yourself to Eleanor Roosevelt, Johanna? What have *you* ever accomplished that would make your life worthwhile?"

That was when it hit Jo that . . . the voice didn't sound at all like Evan's. It wasn't the *sound* of the voice that was wrong. With a whisper, you couldn't tell much. But . . . he was phrasing things differently than Evan, using words and phrases Evan would never use.

But . . . when she'd gone into the bathroom, Evan had been the only person in her room. And they'd driven here in *his* car.

"Did you push me through that glass door at Missy's?" she asked. It was something she needed to know.

"Of course not!" The whisper was deeply offended. "You fell, that's all. I don't *hurt* people, Jo. I *save* them. I was as upset when you fell as you were, because I knew what I'd have to do, and I didn't want to. You have to understand why I'm doing this, Johanna."

Evan never called her Johanna. Never.

"It's important to me that you understand.

I've always liked you. You're very pretty, and you're smart, too. Just what the world needs. But then you went and messed up your face. That was very upsetting to me. At first, I believed what the doctor said, that you'd be 'good as new.' But then I realized the doctor was wrong. You'd never be the same again. So I had no choice. I have my mission. I have to see to it that there is no more ugliness in this world. Can't you understand that?"

Jo's jaw jutted forward. "No. I can't understand that. What gives you the right to say who can live and who can't?"

The voice behind the black ski mask rose to a louder, hoarse whisper. "I'll *tell* you why I have the right!"

And he did.

He told her the story of his life.

Chapter 23

My parents waited a long time to have a child. They wanted everything to be perfect. Perfect jobs, perfect house in the country, perfect peace and quiet and stability for Their perfect child.

And when I was born, I had ten perfect fingers and ten perfect toes and a perfect intellect. Not a thing wrong with my mind.

But the whole left side of my face was covered with a repulsive, shocking-red stain, as if I'd been dipped in berry juice.

I can't even imagine the shock and horror They must have felt. They'd waited so long for me, and They'd expected so much. They must have been heartbroken.

But They didn't reject me, as some parents would have. They didn't turn Their backs on Their imperfect child.

They took me home and raised me. But They were smart enough to know that the world would not be kind to a grotesquely disfigured child. So I was educated at home. I was kept safe and protected in that big white house. I never saw the light of day, never went out of that house until it was dark outside. Summer days were the worst, because it didn't get dark until so late, and it was hot and stuffy inside. Summer days were so long. And so lonely.

Then, when I was twelve, the miracle happened. My mother read about a new technique in the treatment of my kind of disfigurement, a new laser surgery.

And it worked.

Suddenly, the child for whom my parents had waited so long was the child They'd dreamed of. A perfect, flawless, beautiful child. Because underneath the stain, my features were excellent. And I've done everything possible to enhance them.

My parents sold Their house and took me to a small community where no one knew Them. I went out into the world for the first time, and I was accepted totally, without question, just as if I always had been part of the world. My new life was happy and pleasant. So many new things to see and hear and learn about. Happiness was a little bit strange, after so many years without it . . . almost painful, in a way. Hard to adjust to.

I didn't blame my parents for those twelve years of lonely isolation. I knew They were right. The world wouldn't have been kind to my kind of ugliness. And the pain of the world's cruelty would have been unbearable.

They saved me from that.

I realized then that my mission in life was to spare other people with similar, unfortunate deformities from the harsh reality of taunts and teasing and discrimination. I would save them, as I had been saved.

But for a long time, there was no opportunity to fulfill that mission. My parents watched me night and day, as if at any moment, They expected the horrible stain to reappear and ruin everything. I worked really hard at looking perfect every moment of the day, to set Their minds at ease. I could never relax and let myself go, the way other people did, no matter how much I wanted to. They would have worried.

Finally, it was time for college. There wasn't any college or university in the small town where we lived. They couldn't keep me at home, deprive me of the education my fine mind deserved. So They had to let go. They weren't happy about it. They seemed nervous, almost as if They had read my mind and knew what I was planning.

But, of course, that's ridiculous. They couldn't have known.

Their eyes were worried when I left, but I was smiling. I was about to get my chance to fulfill my mission.

Someday, I'll tell Them what I've done. I'll share with Them what I learned from being hidden away from the world for twelve long and lonely years, and how grateful I am to Them for protecting me. Then I'll explain about the mission and how I accomplished what I set out to do, whenever the opportunity presented itself.

They might not understand at first. But I can make Them understand. And when They do, They'll be so proud.

After all, I'm only following Their example, right? I'm only doing what I was taught. By Them.

So how can They not be proud?

Chapter 24

"You can't really think your parents would be proud of you," Jo said with contempt. "You . . . *killed* someone!"

"I *saved* someone!" the voice hissed. "*They'll* see that, even if *you're* too stupid to see it! I saved Sharon, the way They saved me all those years when I was ugly and disgusting."

Jo stood up, still holding the stick. "I'm sorry you went through all that," she said, wrapping her arms around her chest for warmth. "But your parents would have done you a bigger favor if they'd let you out in the world, no matter what your face looked like. Sure, some people would have been cruel, especially little kids and stupid grown-ups. But other people would have been nice. You would have learned to deal with your birthmark. Your parents never gave you the chance."

"Don't you *dare* criticize Them! They were

protecting me! And that's what I did for Sharon, and what I'm doing for you." The whisper became a sob. "God, I wish you'd understand, Jo. I really want you to."

The figure in black bent to pick up a shovel stuck in the overturned earth, and began to move toward Jo.

She understood immediately that she had no more time. She could scream, but they were on the edge of campus, and no one would hear her.

But there had to be something. . . . She couldn't just let him kill her. It couldn't happen. Not, she thought grimly, without a fight.

The whisper, when it came, caught her off guard. "I can't do it. I can't kill you, Jo. I know it's the right thing to do, but it's harder than I thought it would be. I didn't even *know* Sharon, so that was different." Tears sounded in the voice. "What am I going to *do*? I can't just let you go." The whisper became a tortured wail. "I don't know what to *do*!"

The moment's hesitation gave Jo the opportunity she'd been waiting for. She whirled, planning to race away. But she had been kneeling too long, and the cold had slowed her circulation. She stumbled and hadn't taken more than two steps forward when there was a hissed curse of anger from behind her and something cold and hard slammed against her skull.

Knocked off-balance, she tumbled sideways into the waiting hole.

Chapter 25

The earth in the hole was cold and damp. Stunned, Jo lay on the bottom, too dazed to think or feel.

Above her, a voice cried, "You *made* me do that! You were going to run! Now I have to finish the job, Johanna. For a minute there, I almost forgot my mission, and how important it is. If you hadn't tried to run, I might have let you go. Then I'd be a failure. I could never live with that, never."

A shower of dirt descended upon Jo, then another and another. It fell on her back, her legs, her head. She could feel it in her hair. It was surprisingly warm, a blanket of earth that felt almost comforting when she was so very cold.

The temptation to lie there, unresisting, to let the warm, soft dirt cover her up, warm her frozen bones, lasted only a second. Terrified by the thought of giving in, Jo forced herself up on her elbows, then to a sitting position. Earth continued to cascade down upon her, clinging to her gray sweatshirt and jeans.

Then the voice above her changed, began speaking softly as the figure in black shoveled scoop after scoop of dirt and tossed it into the hole. The voice was too soft to recognize, and the words made no sense.

"Hidden . . . hidden away . . . didn't belong out in the world . . . Peter, Peter, Pumpkin Eater, had a wife and couldn't keep her, put her in a pumpkin shell, and there he kept her very well . . . I was in a pumpkin shell and there I kept *me* very well. No," the voice became mournful, "*not* so well. Wanted to be *outside* . . . outside, with people and voices and things to do . . . but They said no, no, no, that wouldn't be good, not good at all, had to stay in pumpkin shell." Grunting now with the effort of shoveling, the voice became ragged, the breathing uneven, but still it kept talking, rambling . . . "dipped in berry juice, *not* perfect, *not* perfect, bad child, bad child, go to your room and stay there for twelve years . . . play hide and seek with *yourself*, no one wants you, no one wants to have to look at you, bad child, bad child. . . ."

Jo pulled herself to her feet. Standing upright brought her chin to the top of the hole. She could hoist herself up. But he would knock her right back in, and this time a blow with the shovel might do more than stun her.

Her stick . . . where was her writing stick?

Still in her left hand. What instinct had kept her from dropping it when she fell?

The voice began singing softly, eerily, "I am my sunshine, my only sunshine." Shoveling, shoveling. The arms in the black jacket had become careless, heedlessly tossing dirt left and right now, much of it missing the hole, and still the voice kept rambling, singing, murmuring to itself.

He doesn't know what he's doing, Jo thought, watching in bewilderment. He's forgotten about me . . . he's lost in his own little world now.

Something on the ground behind him glittered silvery in the light from the Quad's many windows. Keys . . . the car keys . . . he must have dropped them in his haste to pick up the shovel. Keeping her eyes on the softly ranting, shoveling figure, Jo lifted her arm, stretched it out, stick in hand, and strained to make contact with the keys. It took her three tries. Twice, she stopped breathing when the soft singing paused. She froze, afraid he had heard her stick scratching in the dirt. Each time, the singing resumed without a turn of his head.

The third time, the keys caught on the end of the stick, and, holding her breath, she slowly, carefully, dragged them backward until they were close enough to be caught up in her hand. As quickly and quietly as possible, she slid them into her jeans pocket.

But she was still in the hole. The keys did her no good as long as she was standing in a hole more than five feet deep. She had to get out before he came back to reality and remembered why she was there.

"Nobody loves me, everybody hates me, guess I'll go eat worms," singing, shoveling, shoveling, faster and faster but still carelessly, not even looking down at Jo, not checking to see if the hole was filling up ". . . not many games you can play alone, can't play tic-tactoe alone, can't play checkers alone, can't play charades alone, always wanted to play charades, looked like fun on television, no one to play it with . . . bad, bad child, go to your room and stay there. . . ."

In spite of the careless aim of the shovel, the hole was filling up rapidly. Dirt crawled up to Joe's kneecaps, warming her legs. She was afraid to move, to call attention to herself now that he seemed so unaware of her. But if she stayed where she was. . . .

"Hot . . . it's hot . . . so hot in my room . . . summer days are so long." Singing again, "I am my sunshine, my only sunshine. . . ."

Watching the black-clad figure carelessly shoveling scoop after scoop of dirt, muttering and murmuring, singing softly in that eerie off-key monotone, Jo flashed on what it must have been like for the small child hidden away in a room throughout years of long, hot summer days, and she felt a sudden flash of rage against the people responsible. *He* said they'd been protecting him, and really seemed to believe it. But he'd probably *had* to believe it, so that he wouldn't have to hate the only two people in his tiny little world.

Whatever he said he believed, there *was* rage there. She could hear it in the disjointed singing and murmuring. That rage had made him kill once, and was making him kill again now.

In spite of her fear, in spite of her anger at what was being done to her, she felt a terrible pain in her heart, as if an arrow had suddenly pierced it. She could see a small child, confined to his room for years, alone and lonely, feeling like a freak because of an accident of birth. Something that wasn't his fault. But . . . he'd probably thought it was.

The arms began shoveling furiously. "It's hot, it's so hot. . . ." The jacket was shed, tossed on the ground as the exertion raised body temperature in spite of the cold. The voice became the whimper of a small child. "Mommy, please, can I go outside? It's so hot in here. I won't let anyone see me, I promise. I'll stay in the backyard and hide behind the bushes and the trees, please, Mommy, please? It's so hot. . . ."

The childish pleading brought tears to Jo's eyes. God, hadn't they *known* what they were doing, how much damage they were doing?

Suddenly, crying out once again that it was "so hot!" the black-gloved hands reached up to rip off the black ski mask and toss it to the ground.

Silvery-blonde curls rippled to the shoulders.

Perfect, full, red lips smiled to be free of the heavy woolen mask.

Perfect, doe-shaped, turquoise blue eyes turned toward Jo, widening in surprise as if they had forgotten she was there.

Perfect, porcelain skin gleamed in the moonlight.

Forgetting her own plight, Jo's mouth

dropped open and she drew in her breath sharply.

That flawless, perfect oval of a face with its silvery hair and eyes the color of the ocean and skin as smooth as porcelain, belonged to . . .

Nan.

Chapter 26

Jo's mind struggled to take in what it was seeing.

Nan? Beautiful, flawless Nan had been the child hidden away for years because of a disfiguring birthmark?

"Oh," Nan said softly, gazing down at Jo with clouded eyes, "*you're* here. I'd forgotten." Her eyes cleared as she snapped back to reality. "What are you staring at?" And then, as if she'd read Jo's mind, "I *told* you, I had it removed. When I was twelve. Don't you remember?"

The relief that Jo's captor wasn't Evan . . . wasn't, wasn't, wasn't Evan, was short-lived as the look of confusion on Nan's face was quickly replaced by one of determination.

"You draped my mirrors?" Jo asked hastily, hoping to stall for time. "That was you?"

Nan leaned on the shovel. "I used the black

cape that came with that fuschia dress, the one I wore to Missy's party. I told you the dress came with a cape. It was ugly, but I wanted the dress, so . . ." Nan's upper lip curled slightly. "That cape had ugly big gold buttons on it. *Ruined* the look. Some designers do not understand the first thing about perfection. I didn't mind cutting up that cape, not one little bit."

"Where did you get the ski mask?" Jo still had the keys to Evan's car in her pocket. She could feel them burning into her leg. If Nan noticed they were missing. . . .

"At the costume shop, silly. I went down by myself while you were still in the infirmary. That's how I knew there was a Marie Antoinette costume there. Then I was afraid the manager would say something when I came back with you and Kelly. But she didn't even remember me. Kind of insulting, if you ask me. Most people who see me remember me." She laughed bitterly. "But now it's because I'm beautiful, not because I'm a freak."

Jo edged closer to the corner of the trench. If she could distract Nan's attention somehow, she could hoist a leg up and climb out of the hole. "But you're driving *Evan's* car. That's why I was sure you were Evan."

Nan laughed again. "I can't believe you

thought I was Evan. He'd never hurt you. He's nuts about you. Anyone can see that. You should be more trusting, Johanna. Of course, it's too late now."

"Where *is* Evan?" she demanded. "What have you done to him?"

"Nothing. Just bopped him on the head, that's all. He's in your closet. Honestly, Jo, you really should hang your clothes according to color. How do you ever *find* anything in there? Then I borrowed his keys. He won't mind." Suddenly, Nan's voice changed, became crisper, colder. "Enough talk. I almost forgot why I was here. Let's get cracking, and get this over with. You must be really cold. You haven't been working like *I* have." She laughed then, a brief, mirthless sound that echoed across the construction site. "Well, you won't feel the cold much longer, I promise you."

"Nan, don't do this," Jo pleaded as a shovelful of dirt was tossed into the hole. "Dr. Trent says my face is going to look good as new. You don't have to worry about me offending people, or that my feelings will be hurt by things people say."

"She lied," Nan said flatly, continuing to shovel. "The good doctor lied. Your face is going to be seriously flawed. Can't have that, can we?" She stopped and leaned on the shovel.

"Listen, Jo, I'm doing you a favor. You wouldn't be happy living in this world with ugly scars on your face. It's too hard. This world likes pretty things. Trust me, I know. I'm your friend, and I'm going to save you from finding out what it's really like to be . . . different. You should thank me, Jo. You really should." Then she resumed shoveling.

Jo, shivering with cold again, sagged against the earthen wall. It was no use. She wasn't going to talk her way out of this. There was no moving Nan. She had a mission, and she had every intention of fulfilling it. She didn't see it as an act of cruelty. Her sick mind saw it as an act of kindness.

The sharp-pointed writing stick was still in Jo's hand.

"Nan," she called softly, "I have a last wish. Can I tell you my last wish? You wouldn't let me die without at least hearing it, would you?"

Nan paused. She turned to face Jo. "Look, if you're afraid that I'm going to bury you alive, relax. I wouldn't do something so nasty. I'll . . . I'll see to it that you don't know what's happening to you, okay? It won't be so bad, you'll see."

She's going to kill me with that shovel before she buries me, Jo thought, sickened. "One last wish," she repeated insistently. "That's all I'm asking."

Nan looked down at her regretfully. "I wish I didn't have to do this at all, Jo. You were always really nice to me. Lots of girls aren't. They're intimidated by my looks, and don't even try to get to know me." She sighed heavily, her lovely face a study in concentration. "Okay, I guess I owe you that much. One last wish. What is it?"

Jo barely whispered her answer.

"What?" Nan moved closer. "I can't hear you." She sank to her knees beside the trench. "What? What *is* your last wish?"

Jo brought the stick out from behind her and thrust her arm upward, aiming blindly.

The stick raked Nan's cheek from just below the eye to the edge of her chin, leaving a deep scratch, which quickly reddened with a trail of blood.

Although she cried out in pain, shock kept her frozen in place, one hand on her bloody cheek, for several seconds. Her eyes on Jo were full of disbelief.

Then she grasped what had been done to her, and the look turned to one of horror. She jumped up, screaming hysterically, "My face, my face! What have you *done*?" She began staggering about blindly, both hands shielding the injury, as if by hiding it she could make it disappear.

Jo knew this was her chance, probably her only one. The fury in Nan's eyes . . . any moment now, she would turn to vent that rage, and there'd be no stopping her this time.

Fueled by fear, Jo was up and over the edge of the trench and stumbling, running on cold, stiff legs, before Nan had turned around.

It was hard to negotiate the upturned earth. Twice, Jo stumbled and nearly fell.

Behind her, she heard an oath, and a shouted, "You'll *pay* for this. You'll pay . . ."

But Jo reached the car first, yanked the keys from her pocket, pulled the door open, and jumped into the driver's seat. The smell of Evan made her eyes water. Was he okay?

She started the engine, switched on the headlights. Here came Nan, lurching over the rutted earth, her face bloody, her eyes wild.

Jo's hands were shaking so badly, they kept slipping off the steering wheel.

Nan raced toward the car.

Jo could *feel* the hatred and fury heading straight for her.

Unseeing in her terror, she threw the car into gear and stomped down hard on the gas.

It raced forward.

And Nan ran to meet it, her bloody face

twisted in rage, her arms outstretched as if to stop the car.

There was no way of stopping in time.

The thud was sickening.

Jo screamed.

Her hands left the wheel and flew up to cover her eyes as Nan's body was thrown up over the hood and into the windshield. Her head struck the glass with a sharp cracking sound. The impact bounced her back off the car again, up into the air and then down.

She came to rest on the only patch of grass that hadn't been destroyed by construction vehicles.

Her arms and legs flopped lifelessly as she landed. Then she lay still and silent.

Chapter 27

Jo never knew who called the police. She was only vaguely aware that people were around her, as if she were seeing them through a thick gauze curtain. They were gently helping her out of Evan's car, they were wrapping a heavy jacket around her, they were leading her to the infirmary. Dr. Trent was there, peering into her face again, bringing her hot coffee, wrapping her in blankets. It was Dr. Trent who told her that Nan was alive, after all. In bad shape physically as well as emotionally, but alive. It would be a long time before she would be okay, a very long time.

"But," the doctor added, "with a lot of help, she'll make it."

And then, after a·while, Evan was there, too, an egg-shaped patch of dried blood on his left temple, asking her over and over again if she was all right.

She didn't know. Nothing seemed right. Nothing seemed real.

Kelly arrived, her eyes swollen from crying, in shock over Nan. She kept whispering, "I can't believe it, I can't believe it."

Jo had told the police where to find Sharon Westover. One policeman had returned to thank her and tell her that Sharon's body would be sent home now, to her family.

Dr. Trent led Kelly away to treat her for shock, and Jo and Evan were left alone in the small white cubicle.

"Quit that," Evan said quietly. He leaned down very close to Jo and took both her hands in his. "Quit feeling guilty because you thought it was me. I don't blame you."

Jo felt herself flushing. "You knew?"

He nodded. "The look on your face when that pink receipt fell out of my wallet was a dead giveaway. And I can just imagine what you thought when you realized you were being taken away in *my* car." He smiled down at her. "Now you're thinking that you should have trusted me, and how could you have possibly thought that someone as wonderful as me could do those awful things, right?"

"I didn't *want* to think it was you," Jo said. "I wanted to trust you."

"Not your fault. You don't know me well

enough to trust me." His smile broadened. "But you're going to. You *can* trust me on that one."

Nan . . . poor, twisted Nan . . . had told Jo that she needed to be more trusting.

Now seemed like a good time to begin.